subversion

T. A. Alderson

broadway books
new york

subversion

A ROMANTIC
SUSPENSE STORY

SUBVERSION. Copyright © 2001 by T. A. Alderson. All rights reserved. Printed in the United States of America. No part of this book may be reproduced or transmitted in any form or by any means, electronic or mechanical, including photocopying, recording, or by any information storage and retrieval system, without written permission from the publisher. For information, address Broadway Books, a division of Random House, Inc., 1540 Broadway, New York, NY 10036.

Broadway Books titles may be purchased for business or promotional use or for special sales. For information, please write to: Special Markets Department, Random House, Inc., 1540 Broadway, New York, NY 10036.

BROADWAY BOOKS and its logo, a letter B bisected on the diagonal, are trademarks of Broadway Books, a division of Random House, Inc.

Visit our website at www.broadwaybooks.com

Library of Congress Cataloging-in-Publication Data

Alderson, T. A., 1955–
Subversion: a romantic suspense story / T. A. Alderson.—1st ed.
　p.　cm.
　1. Women lawyers—Fiction.　2. Washington (D.C.)—Fiction.
　I. Title.
PS3551.L3369 S8 2001
813'.6—dc21　　　　　　　　　　　　　　　　　　00-057904

FIRST EDITION

Book design by Pei Loi Koay

ISBN 0-7679-0567-8

01　02　03　04　05　10　9　8　7　6　5　4　3　2　1

for Carlina

subversion

that morning I awoke from a dream of death.

In my dream I was leaving the Manhattan offices of my old law firm, taking the elevator down from the forty-seventh floor in the tallest of the International-style cereal boxes that form a phalanx between the World Trade Center and the East River. I wasn't alone in this dream; I rode the elevator with my father, watching him watch the floor numbers flash, noting his impatience to reach the ground. He had no desire to be stuck on an elevator with me. That was clear, even in the murkiness of dream space.

Out on the narrow street the dial car waited. When we slipped into the backseat, I saw that the driver wore dark glasses. Strange, the dark glasses, because it was after midnight, but in this dream-night the light was odd: gelid, white-gold, at once obscurant and illuminating.

In front of us another car blocked the way. There wasn't room to go around. Our driver tapped his horn.

"Take care of it," my father said. Authoritatively, preemptively. Addressing the driver, not me.

Our driver stepped out of the car to confront the other driver. They faced each other briefly in the space between the cars before the other driver pulled a black pistol out of his coat and fired point-blank. Our driver's dark glasses flew off as he fell out of sight. I watched the glasses come to rest on the hood and listened to my waking consciousness remind me, *This isn't happening, this is only a dream.* But the dream kept on.

The other driver shoved his gun through our window. A Charter Arms Bulldog, I noted, and I wanted to tell my father, *See, I know what it is. Look at what I've learned.* But his eyes were on the driver; he was not even aware of my presence. The driver looked like the young Dirk Bogarde; I found myself reflexively pulling back my hair and smiling at him. Flirt, I could feel my father thinking. Slut. The driver shot him. Twice he shot him, then turned the gun on me. The bullets were painless, but I fell forward, watching myself fall, feeling my conscious soul drop through the floor of the car into a black hole lined with geometric shapes—polyhedrons, squares, and spirals—that moved and splintered and coalesced as I plunged through them toward a deep absorbent mass I could sense but not see.

Then I woke up.

I wasn't in Manhattan but in Washington, D.C. The digital clock beside my bed said 5:38 A.M., which meant that in twenty-two minutes the alarm would go off. There are few pleasures as profound as waking up to find you can go back to sleep, but twenty-two minutes is right on the cusp of utility: too short a time to savor leisurely, and too long to ignore without falling back into unconsciousness. I fell back into unconsciousness. When I woke up again, it was after seven. Time to jump and move.

I sat up and put my feet on the floor. Sometimes I thought that was the biggest moment of my day: everything before that action was potentiality and good intention; everything afterward was a grim response to necessity and a losing war with entropic disintegration. I sucked a load of air through my nostrils. I flopped on my back again and bicycled my legs in the air, unhappily aware of the flesh at my waist. Constant vigilance: the purgatory of the metabolically challenged. I spread my legs wide, savoring all of the luxuriant space in my warm bed and thinking how if I really had my freedom I would live in the bed, I'd never get up except to go to the bathroom, I'd sleep eighteen hours a day and burrow deep into the cellar of dreams, where I've always been happiest.

Except what was this with Dirk Bogarde, pointing a gun at my face?

I sat back up. I swiveled on an imaginary fulcrum at the small of my back and vaulted out of bed. All right. I made it to the bathroom and sat down again. Did my morning business and did not step on the scale. Gave myself a break. I had another flash of my father, residue from the dream. I looked in the mirror at my father's eyes, his contribution to my face. A face that could launch armadas, a face that could burn cities. Or so I'd been told by one of my more literary admirers.

"It's a good thing God made you fat," Mother once said to me, "or you'd be more than the world could bear."

Thanks, Mom.

Alpha-hydroxy cream at the corners of my eyes, just a touch of mascara, lipstick in two layers: a burnt umber underneath, followed by a brick-Georgian red I hadn't tried before. The wrinkle cream was a gift for my thirty-second birthday, not that there were any wrinkles visible yet. What I mean to say is that the gift wasn't a hint. I'd asked for it. A thoughtful present from my current employer. And boyfriend. I suppose he was my boyfriend; I guess that's the proper term. I always hated that word, "boyfriend," and I never used to use it. Now it seems I have to say it, if only to limit the come-ons I have to fend off in the course of a day. But that morning I had a boyfriend. Even if I couldn't tell anyone about him. I had a rich boyfriend, a good job, a decent apartment, and the pleasant delusion that I knew the score. I guess I should have stayed in bed.

There were four messages on my answering machine, the same four I'd been too tired to check last night. One from my sister Caroline, thanking me for remembering her son's birthday. One from my friend Valerie, asking me to call her. Then a hang-up. Then another near hang-up, except there was something said. One word, an exclamation. I rewound the tape and listened again.

"Hi, this is Rosalind. You know how to leave a message, don't you? You just put your lips together and—"

Beeeeeeeep.

There were a few seconds of silence, then a quick "Hey" and then the dial tone. The voice was unfamiliar. It almost sounded British.

These hang-ups were irritating me. They were happening almost every day, and I was starting to worry a little. Only I couldn't bother with it right now: I was late for work. And work, for the first time in my life, was not something I dreaded. I power-slurped a cup of coffee, looked out my bay window at the Capitol dome, shredded the plastic around my dry-cleaned suit, and dressed myself. Lawyering. It's a job anyone can do, so appearances are important. I couldn't find any panty hose that weren't full of holes. Shit. I dumped out the overflowing dirty-clothes hamper. No luck. Might as well mine it for tomorrow's underwear, since I was wearing my last clean pair. I needed to get organized. I already had a cleaning woman who came in twice a month. It was time to hire out my laundry, too.

But the panty hose question. I could go bare-legged in my office. It was one of the great things about my job. I'd even get extra points for it. But it was mid-October, past the bare leg season. Plus I had a big bruise on my knee and another one on my thigh. And my boss put them there. Innocently. Consensually, anyway. It would seem best to cover them up, though. Black tights, ideally. They didn't seem available. Was it going to be pants day, then?

I ended up in pants. Black jeans. That was permissible, too, as long as there was no client contact. And I didn't expect any today. There was a big meeting in New York, but that was tomorrow. I'd buy hose tonight and look good for the Metroliner ride in the morning. I grabbed my Export As, my last box.

Out the door and down the stairs, five flights of them, and out into a fine autumn day. The leaves along East Capitol Street were in their first fall turning. I strolled across Third Street, headed toward the Capitol, past the Folger on my left, coming up on Second Street and the back of the Supreme Court Building. I took a right. This was a long-cherished fantasy: being able to walk to work. Down a long block of tall narrow Capitol Hill row houses, down to the corner confluence of Constitution and Maryland Avenues, to the handsome pink brick edifice with the imposing wood panel door and the discreet brass plate, no bigger than a postcard, announcing the office of Rigel Associates. My firm. I was house counsel. "House counsel of Rigel Associates." I loved saying that. In Washington, where there is no conversation apart from "What do you do?," it was a golden answer to every question.

And it *was* a house—the office had once been somebody's very comfortable house. No lobby, no elevator ride. I stepped through the door right into the reception area and said good morning to the Australian babe at the front desk. "Good morning, Miss Wilcox." She was hired for her accent. Not quite BBC, but better than homegrown. Always called me Miss Wilcox. I loved that, too.

My office was on the first floor, looking out on a thickly overgrown garden where ivy trellises filtered the light and blocked any visual evidence of the twentieth century. All I could see was part of the aged brick back of a neighboring row house. There was a stone bench out there, where, I'm sorry to report, I once engaged in some unprofessional conduct. But now I faced more professional demands, for when I logged on to my computer there was already a summons to come upstairs and see Lucius Atkinson, one of the partners. Not the partner with whom I was unprofessionally involved. His name was Marshall Waverly. He was at that moment in Los Angeles. In the airport. Thinking of me, no doubt.

So it was upstairs to the second floor. First I peeked into Claudia's office—Claudia Austen, Swarthmore dropout, U. Va. graduate, and administrative assistant.

"Where'd you go last night?" I asked.

"Tiber Rio."

"No." Tiber Rio was a Hill margarita bar stuffed with Senate staff Pop-Tarts just waiting to be eaten.

"Afraid so."

"Any luck?"

"Afraid so."

"Sorry."

"Lucius is waiting for you."

"I know."

"Is there a problem?"

"Probably."

"Probably."

"I'll see you."

"You go, girl."

I did. I stood in front of Lucius Atkinson's desk with a scowl on my face and my hand on my hip. You could still see the hippie he'd been, in spite of the two-thousand-dollar suit and the four-hundred-dollar shoes. Like a sizable subset of his generation, he'd made an intellectual journey from Marx to de Maistre, and it manifested itself in a desire to make huge sums of money on Wall Street.

"What's up?"

He tapped his keyboard and swiveled toward me, putting his feet up on the desk. "South Africa," he said.

"What about it?"

"They don't like your draft."

"Well, fuck 'em."

"They're not going to agree to the terrorism covenants."

"Then don't sign it."

"We want to do the deal."

"You're going to get screwed. It's a lousy contract."

"What if I told you there were other considerations?"

"I'd tell you to get another lawyer."

He sighed, puffing out his cheeks. "They don't want to have to pay for any delays in power delivery due to sabotage."

"So who is going to pay? De Beers?"

"They don't think there's going to be any sabotage."

"Then it shouldn't be an issue for them."

He puffed out his cheeks again. "Look, can you just redraft the thing without clause 7a? Just for now?"

"Sure. I'll call Winslow this morning. It's just billable time as far as they're concerned. What do they care if we lose our knickers?"

Winslow, Cooper, and Stowe was our outside counsel. My old firm in New York. They had a Washington office.

"Good. And one more thing."

"What?"

"Check the Swiss escrow account. Van Zyk owes us money. He says he paid it. Yesterday."

"Yesterday. Check's in the mail."

"It should be in the account. If you could just make sure."

"All right."

"Marshall's coming in this afternoon. We may have a meeting."

I didn't allude to my precise knowledge of when Marshall was arriving, or mention that I might be meeting him at the airport. Our relationship was a secret. The best kind. You want to make love last, keep it hidden.

"Okay."

"Okay."

I stopped back in on Claudia. She had her head on her desk.

"Wake up, lovergirl."

"I've got to cut this out," she said. "Should I go to law school?"

"No. Absolutely not. Emphatically no."

"That's what I thought. But I've got to do something."

"You're twenty-three."

"Four."

"Twenty-four. The best age on earth. Enjoy it."

Her phone rang. She yawned and waved bye-bye with wiggling fingers. I went downstairs to my office. I closed the door and lit my first cigarette of the day. Not bad. I managed to avoid having a wake-up smoke with my coffee. My new tobacco-reduction program, to go with my new weight-loss program and my get-organized program and my keep-my-apartment-tidy program and my be-faithful-to-my-boyfriend program. How many of these programs would I fall off of by sundown?

On my screen, a program dedicated to tracking capital flows opened with a dollar-sign icon. Capital flow. It governed everything now. It was the mind of God. Sure, people lived and died, loved, hated, sought the Great Spirit, climbed mountains, wrote novels, structured leasebacks under Delaware law, accepted Jesus as their personal Lord and Savior, held AK-47s aloft in the name of Allah—but only one thing really mattered: capital flow. So I typed in commands faster than I could think them, my hands moving out of long reflexive habit, out of the same unconscious nervous impulses that made my diaphragm rise and fall. But something was wrong. Something was irrevocably out of joint. I tapped the keyboard with increasing agitation, but the results scrolled impassively down the screen, row after row of zero balances. I reentered the query, I checked the account numbers, I exited the program and started from the beginning. But the answer was the same.

The Banca della Svizzera Italiana account was empty.

The cursor sat where I'd left it, blinking in the southeast corner of the screen, stupidly, insistently. I looked out at the overgrown garden, at the stone bench, and thought of vacation. Getting away. A stream of images from past Mediterranean and Caribbean escapes: white beaches, tall cool drinks . . . second-floor *pensione* rooms overlooking enclosed stone courtyards . . . Nino . . . vaporetto rides to the Lido . . . languid afternoons of unhurried sex. I thought of how many such afternoons $3.7 million could buy. Before I buzzed Lucius with the bad news, I let myself enjoy one more cigarette.

what do you do when you know there's nothing you want to do?

You go to law school.

It's what I did. It's what everyone I knew did. It's what my whole generation did. And I did it in spite of my avowals to friends, in spite of my undergraduate contempt for the prospect, in spite of the skull-imploding expense.

And four years into a big-firm career, I wanted out.

I considered a lot of alternatives. Did you know the FBI wants lawyers? That's right. Lawyers and accountants. Tough guys are passé. They want Agent Scully. I inquired, went to a preliminary interview. But I knew the FBI and I wouldn't get along. And there was the question of my daddy. I really didn't care to discuss his case with some G-man personnel prick. So that was out.

I looked at some public-interest jobs, but after a few interviews with the same earnest beard-and-backpack wieners I'd hated in college, I gave that up. The only reason I'd ever go out with a guy sporting a ponytail is so I could cut it off in his sleep. Forget that.

Capitol Hill. I checked it out. I give a superlative blow job when I want to, but I don't fancy having it part of my official duties. Good-bye to that.

I was thinking of mail-order courses in how to become a Saab mechanic when the partner I did most of my work for brought my attention to a tiny item in the back of *American Lawyer*. "Small boutique investment firm seeks in-house counsel with project finance, capital markets experience. Work directly for principals in dynamic, intimate setting." Six to eight years' experience, they said, but what the hell. I'd give it a try. Five years was close to six; perhaps I'd impress them on the interview. I'd done well at firm presentations: they don't call those things beauty contests for nothing.

And I did impress them. Eventually. At first I wasn't sure how it would go. I didn't know what to make of Lucius Atkinson. We didn't meet in some fortieth-floor corporate aerie. We met down in SoHo, at a slick joint on Mercer Street. A lot of models used to go there, I think. We sat at a table in the back of the blue-lit room, next to the stairs to the mezzanine where the bathrooms were. Everyone going up to take a piss was on display for the whole room; in fact, the toilets themselves were on display: there was some special glass in the doors that became opaque only when you closed them. Lucius didn't pay any attention to the finely toned calves that were flexing up and down the stairs. He appeared to have eyes only for me. We drank Bombay Sapphire martinis, and I told him about the deals I'd worked on and the credit agreements I'd drafted and the negotiations I'd participated in.

"You're from Zanesville, Ohio," he said.

"Yes." I almost added, *Is that a problem?*

"You went to Kenyon."

"Yes."

"John Crowe Ransom. Robert Lowell."

"Yes. Way back when. The college is cruising on the memory."

"Is Dr. Robert Wilcox your father?"

I couldn't believe it. Dad was big news around Zanesville, but only a brief blip on the national news radar. They'd been checking on me. I guess if they weren't already interested, they never would have bothered. I looked around at the beautiful people gassing away, at the delectably unshaven bartender, at the door to Mercer Street, where I suddenly wanted to be.

"Yes, he is."

"When's the last time you saw him?"

"It's been over four years now."

"Do you know where he is?"

"No one does."

He nodded. "I'm sorry," he said.

"It's all right. We live with it."

"We?"

"My family."

"Right."

Down the stairs came somebody I recognized, somebody sort of famous that I couldn't immediately place. I was waiting for the horseshit "interview" questions, the *Where do you see yourself in five years?* and the *If you had to describe your greatest weakness, what would it be?* and the *Why do you want to work for Rigel Associates?* They never came, and by the time we walked out on Mercer Street, I knew I wanted this gig. But Atkinson was a sphinx, even after three drinks, and he said I needed to meet with his partner, Marshall Waverly. Could I come down to Washington?

I could. We had lunch at the Hay-Adams Hotel, then took a taxi up Connecticut Avenue to the firm's tiny branch office on Calvert Street. That, I eventually learned, amounted to Marshall's private office. There, in a lucky coincidence of interests, I secured the job.

Marshall was a gun nut. Not a redneck, jacked-up four-wheeler, camouflage-headband nut. A different kind of nut. He was an urbane Virginia gentleman, and I would have assumed his interest in firearms would not extend beyond a Holland & Holland over-and-under. But somehow we got onto the subject of Israel, and Israel's role in the international arms trade, and then onto the virtues of Israeli assault rifles. And this was a subject I knew something about.

I'd actually fired a Galil. That got his attention. And I went into a whole assault-rifle riff, how I preferred the .308 to the .223, how much I hated the fussy, schoolmarmish M-16, how much I loved the classic, redolent-of-colonialism

FN-FAL, how easy it was to fieldstrip an AK, with its indestructible bolt. It was a million-dollar trove of trivia, it turned out. It had just been sitting uselessly in the back of my head for over ten years. I looked into Marshall Waverly's eyes. I'd seen that expression before. Many times. He was mine.

How did I know that boy stuff? The answer was back in Zanesville, back in strip-mine afternoons with my high school buddy Drew Gillespie, the boy I thought was incompatible with my rise out of small-town Ohio, the boy I thought I had to say good-bye to for our own good. He owned a Chinese AK, one that would only fire semiauto. I was the bad daughter in my family: my sisters were outraged by guns and hunting, as if they were already the East Coast graduates of the Ivy League most of them eventually became. That was why I was down in the mine, blowing cans off the rock face: because my sisters never would be. And after Kenyon, in the summer of 1988, I saw Drew for what I thought would be the last time. But before we had our unhappy final chat of the season, we shot all his new rifles: the AR-15, the Valmet, the Galil. I owed this job to Drew.

Who looked, by the way, like a Buckeye version of that Mercer Street bartender. And who stayed in the back of my mind, sometimes making his way to the front at inopportune moments.

I was so relaxed after my firearms disquisition that I did the unthinkable:

"Do you mind if I smoke?"

"Not at all."

I made a show of taking out my Canadian cigarettes. Marshall reached across his desk to offer his Dunhill.

"Amazing," I said. "No one has a lighter anymore."

"A certain tedious sanctimony has become very fashionable."

I felt my lips stretching involuntarily from an O of exhalation into a smile of pure joy. Things had taken a turn. For the better. Not only did I have a new job, I was almost in love again.

the surreptitious romantic reunion I'd been envisioning was not to be. Lucius actually had me by the arm, dragging me down the Metro escalator at Union Station. He and Marshall had decreed a war council at the Calvert Street office. So I was going to have to be on my best behavior. All business. It was quite a disappointment.

"Shit, I don't have a Farecard," said Lucius.

"I told you to take a taxi."

"Cost cutting."

"Oh, yeah. Four million dollars disappears and you're worrying about taxi fare."

In front of us a wide black woman inserted a five-dollar bill in the fare machine, had it rejected, inserted it again, had it rejected again, finally inserted it successfully and then laboriously punched the minus-value button until the minimum fare registered and a cascade of change clanged into a bin. My boy Lucius was apoplectic at the end of this performance, during which a Red Line train arrived and departed without us.

"Another day in Uganda-on-the-Potomac," Lucius said.

"Relax."

"Easy for you to say. You don't have an equity stake in this transaction."

"But I have an emotional stake. I'm a loyal employee."

He looked me in the eye, for the first time since I gave him the news. "Good. You don't know how important that's going to be."

At Woodley Park we rode up the long escalator in silence. Lucius stood sideways on the moving steps, staring at the opposite wall. This was abnormal. Usually he was a talk box. I had no trouble imagining him back at Columbia with Mark Rudd, his megaphone spewing like a foundry chimney. He loved to lecture me. Whether he wanted to sleep with me as well was yet to be definitively determined.

"You been going to the gym?" he suddenly asked.

Men would be perfect, I've decided, if they just had a mute button in the small of their backs. Women complain that men won't talk, but in my experience they won't shut up. Maybe it's me.

"Semiannually."

"You look good."

"Hey, fuck you."

It's funny, but I never spoke that way to Marshall. My lover. He was too polite, and I didn't want to let him down. I wanted to live up to some Charlottesville standard of good deportment. I was always throttling my temper in his presence, beating down the Zanesville mall rat who kept threatening to burst out of her Ann Taylor and pearl-bracelet bonds. With Lucius, I didn't make the effort.

"Fuck . . . you," I reiterated, slowly and quietly.

We walked down Connecticut Avenue, through the welter of Indian, Thai, Vietnamese, Mexican, Lebanese, and Italian restaurants. At the corner of Calvert I felt the Baskin-Robbins calling to me, summoning the mall rat from her cave. Luckily there was no chance of stopping.

"Well, fuck you, too," Lucius said. It was gratifying, dragging him down to my level.

We crossed Connecticut, heading toward Adams-Morgan. Our uptown office was in the first block of Calvert, in another old row house. There was no receptionist here, no sign indicating a connection to Rigel. But Marshall had a separate computer up here, one whose files I'd never seen, and a fax machine connected to a scrambler. I wondered what else was up here.

"How was your trip?" That was Lucius, opening the meeting.

"Unpleasant," said Marshall. I'd only nodded at him. He was a tall man, with graying blond hair, and he was pretty fit for his age. He had a very straight nose that I was very fond of. But now he looked tired, and I wanted to kiss him. I wanted to improve his mood. I knew what he needed, after the mirror-glass hell of Century City, after the traffic on

Santa Monica Boulevard. What he didn't need was this meeting.

"So we've been robbed," he said.

"Or there's been a mistake."

"No mistake. Unless we made it. No one has the account access code but us. The three of us."

"I tried to call Van Zyk," I said. He was the South African client who had promised to make a payment into the Swiss account. "He seems to be unavailable."

"I'll handle him," Marshall said.

"What we need you to do," said Lucius, referring to me, "is get over to Winslow and revise the contract."

"I talked to them."

"Maybe you should drop in on them."

"Okay. Whatever."

I got the feeling he wanted to be rid of me. Marshall was looking at me, nodding in agreement. They seemed to want to be alone.

"What about the Swiss account?" I asked.

They looked at each other. Lucius stared at the ceiling, massaging his throat. Suddenly I felt like the now-superfluous friend at a singles bar, whose companion has found a bedmate and just wants me gone, sweet dreams, she'll tell me about it in the morning.

so I was back out on Connecticut Avenue, alone this time, holding up my hand for a taxi. The Washington office of Winslow, Cooper was down off Farragut Square, on I Street. I dreaded going in there. The old claustrophobic feeling descended on me again as I stepped into the lobby, the gilded postmodern granite-and-marble slave quarters. What a Potemkin facade. Into the elevator: walnut panels, Old World dentils, impress-the-client recessed lighting. Out on the eighth floor, crossing the foyer, a slightly down-market version of the one on Manhattan, the one I'd crossed for five years with the view of New York Harbor, the twin spiral staircases, the Fairfield Porter landscapes, the killer receptionists. I was so glad to be free of that place.

"I'm here to see Barry Weiss."

Half-Smoke, I almost said.

There were two partners in charge of the project finance practice group at Winslow, Cooper, and Stowe. One was known to the associates as K.A., which stood for King Asshole. The other one's name was Super Wiener. Super Wiener was the one who had brought me the *American Lawyer* with the Rigel Associates house counsel ad circled in ink. Guess he wanted to get rid of me. The Wiener's chief acolyte was Barry Weiss, very senior associate, christened Half-Smoke by me because he was a half-assed version of his boss. He was always happy to see me, for all the wrong reasons.

"Rosalind, I'm delighted."

He was looking at my black jeans. Let him envy my freedom.

"I was just passing by and thought I'd drop in."

"It's such a beautiful day."

"I'm thinking about getting a moped. What do you think?"

"Was traffic bad?"

"Terrible."

"Could be worse."

"Yes. Could be L.A."

He'd lost a few pounds since I left the firm. I think he wanted me to notice, because he leaned forward and said:

"What do riding a moped and fucking a fat girl have in common?"

I could have refused to play, but I was curious.

"What?"

"They're both fun as long as no one sees you doing it."

He'd always wanted me. Jokes like that were not helping his quest.

"I want to see what you've done on the Xantex contract."

"I think the simplest solution is just to delete 7a."

"That's not what I want. I want to rewrite 7a."

"Okay. What do you want to say?"

"I want something we can give away if we have to. But I want something."

"Right now it says that Xantex will pay the full cost of obtaining alternate power in the event of a mine shutdown due to power interruption, plus a penalty charge of forty-five percent of the mine's daily revenue stream for every day that operations are disrupted. That's for ordinary operations."

"I'm talking about force majeure."

"In case of a force majeure interruption, the penalty charge is thirty percent."

"The problem is, Xantex wants an exemption for terrorist activity. If some rogue Pygmies blow up the power lines, they don't want to pay."

"Right now you've got them paying thirty percent."

"That's right."

"And they won't sign."

"That's right."

"So what do you want?"

"Make it twenty-five."

"They still won't sign."

"So. Maybe I'll end up getting fifteen. You see what I'm saying?"

"Yes."

"Can I have it tomorrow?"
"You're the boss."
"Don't forget it."

I sat and watched him, waiting for him to tell me something. Something that might help me at the meeting tomorrow in New York. Men were always telling me things. How about this: Late at night, in a conference room after twelve hours of rancorous palaver regarding a deal on a coal-fired power plant in Thailand, I'm sitting with a client. It had been a long and shaky negotiation. The baht had swooped up and down against the dollar, taking us all on a sick-making roller-coaster ride that had—as a collateral matter—nearly sunk one of the advising investment banks. Anyway, there we were, alone, and he just started talking, said too much, went into a rapturous free association wherein he confessed he wanted to try on my stockings. Consequently I was able to bill two weeks' extra time without a peep from him. And this was not an isolated incident. The odd thing was not that perfectly ordinary men had these desires, but that they were willing to tell me about them. Tell *me,* when they would not tell their wives or girlfriends or locker-room buddies. I could always feel it coming on, the trembling preamble as barriers of propriety crumbled and the revelatory rush began. I had an effect on men like sodium pentothal.

Sometimes.

Nothing was happening now.

And nothing had happened back on Calvert Street. They'd wanted me gone. So they could talk privately. What was that all about? Now I was feeling petulant.

"I'm seeing Eric on three deals tomorrow," I said. Eric was Eric Hoffman. Super Wiener. "I don't want to have to spend more than ten minutes on this one."

"It'll be ready."
"It better."
He looked at me. Wait a minute; it was happening.
"Are you seeing anyone?"
"No, Barry."
"Can I call you sometime?"
"I don't think that's a good idea."
"Why not?"
"Because."
"Because we do business."
"That's right."
"You don't date business associates."
"That's right."
Three lies inside of a minute. A personal best.

i was idling on Farragut Square, admiring the watch Marshall gave me, when my cell phone trilled. It was an odd thing for me, standing on the street with a cell phone: I enjoyed it, on the one hand, and loathed myself at the same time. The same way I felt while eating a whole pizza or jumping into the sack with some guy I'd just met. The same way I felt riding in Marshall's Range Rover. Queasy, yet excited.

"Sorry, darling," Marshall said.
"Yeah, well, business is business."
"Come see me."
"Right now?"
"Right now."
"I really should get back over to the Hill."
"No, you're needed here."
"Have you been a bad boy?"
"I have."

So that was it. The agenda for the evening. I wasn't dressed for it, but it didn't matter. My outfit was waiting for me: black gloves, black slingbacks, a red bolero jacket, round Italian sunglasses. Business wear. I aimed my whip at the soles of his feet; if he had trouble walking into his meeting with British Petroleum in the morning, so much the better. Every step would remind him of me.

I'd been sleeping with him for a couple of months before the whipping business ever came up. I was a good sport. It wasn't my first time. I asked him if his wife had serviced him that way, and he said no. There you go. But I have a weakness of my own: seeing the light in their eyes when they find out the answer is yes. That's always been my downfall, my pleasure in that light.

"Shit, I forgot to get stockings," I said, much later, in bed, after wine and flounder and a salad full of Sutton Place leaves and tubers. Unlike me, Marshall could cook. He'd make some woman a fine wife.

"Oh, dear."
"We have those meetings tomorrow."
"Wear a pants suit."
"Either way, I have to go home."
"We should bring more of your stuff up here."

"Since we're not seeing each other, that would strike any observer as odd."

"You're the lawyer."

I stroked his cheek with the whip handle.

"Pay attention to your attorney."

"Tomorrow."

I dressed and looked with only a moment's guilt at the dirty dishes.

"So, Marshall."

"Yes."

"What about the Swiss account?"

"Don't worry about it. It's a clerical problem."

"Clerical problem."

"The money's in another account."

I sat down on the bed.

"What aren't you telling me, sweetheart?"

"Nothing."

"Come on."

Stroking his chest, I thought of how old he was, and how young he looked.

"You know something?" he asked. I kissed his throat. "When Lucius was arrested at Columbia, I was in Laos."

In Vientiane, where you could hire girls to do anything.

"I knew that."

"We're still on different planets."

"What, don't you trust him?"

"I have to trust him."

"Does he have something to do with the empty account?"

"Of course not."

He was fifty-four, fifty-five years old. I thought of Dorian Gray. I couldn't help myself.

my apartment seemed forlorn, sadly postcollegiate, after Marshall's place. No Persian rugs, no ebony lamps, no marvelous inlaid rolltop desk or burled mahogany coffee table so suitable as a chastisement scaffold. No built-in oaken bookshelves. Well, I was still paying off school debts; I'd be free in another month. No hardwood shelving for me. Just some brick-and-board crap, holding up my ratty paperbacks and the handsome bound volumes of the deals I did at

Winslow, with my name embossed in gold on the bindings. Like a high school yearbook. I did have a couple of decent pictures on the walls, not framed-poster schlock, but some original art given to me by the artists. Also a family photograph, taken in 1969 but still black-and-white and respectable-looking: Dad and Mother and the first three of us, Caroline and me and Patricia. The twins came later, in the summer of '71. Pamela and Mary. Five girls in all. In the photograph, I'm sitting on my father's lap. I'm not quite two and a half, wearing an Easter dress and a flat-brimmed straw hat trailing long pink ribbons.

Zanesville. What's to tell? I remember sitting on the sofa at Drew Gillespie's house: Olan Mills family photographs on knotty pine walls, a stack of *Reader's Digest*s by the television set. You just wanted to blow your brains out. From the time I was twelve, I couldn't wait to leave. Now none of us are there; even Mother decamped to Cincinnati and reclaimed her maiden name. A lawyer owns the second house I grew up in, a young lawyer, not much older than I am, married to another lawyer. Small-town yuppies. Yes, such people exist. The first house I lived in is gone.

It was a clapboard bungalow, with a front porch and a big dormer punching out of the long slanted roof. My room, the one I shared with Caroline, was up there against the south face of the roof, looking out over the street. Dad bought it in 1960, the year after he married his young bride, nine years his junior. The money came from her parents. She was barely nineteen. He was twenty-eight, just finishing medical school, and broke. They waited five years to have a child. But once we started coming, we came in bulk. And the five of us were quite a strain on that three-bedroom bungalow. We were happy, though. It was our happiest time. I would keep watch out the dormer window, waiting for Dad to come home, and when his rusting yellow Galaxie 500 pulled up, I would run down to welcome him in. That went on for years, until I was seven and the Galaxie had been replaced by an Olds 98. We moved to our big new house and Dad wasn't home so much and when he did come home he was cranky and walked right past me if I ran to meet him. And past Mom, too. The bad times were coming. They came with the money.

When I was ten, our old bungalow burned down.

Four more messages on my answering machine. One a hang-up. Two telemarketers, just wishing me a happy life and promising to check back at a more convenient time. Shitbirds. Then a message from Valerie: a bulletin from the dating wars, and could we meet for breakfast?

I was chewing my nails again. And I'd been so good the last few months. It was the Swiss account. Something very haywire there. It was stressing me. Sex, a pack of cigarettes, a full dinner, and here I was still dying for something to bite. Luckily my refrigerator was empty.

I thought of my dream. Dirk Bogarde and the gun. The phone rang. When I picked up, the line went dead.

After a few minutes of lying coiled in the fetal position on an afghan knitted by my mother's mother, I went to the closet and pulled down a shoe box. I spread out the three postcards I'd gotten from Drew Gillespie over the last ten years. There was one from the fall of '89, dated the same day the Berlin Wall fell, announcing his engagement to Stephanie Granger. The last time I'd seen her she was a gangly ninth grader with braces, one of those tall girls who hunch their shoulders so they won't tower over those pimple-faced goobers they're foolishly hoping will notice them. On the evidence of the photo Drew sent me, everything had fallen into place five years later. Stephanie was a serious babe, with maybe too much Zanesville big-hair—but then Drew would like that, wouldn't he? But they never did get married. Drew was still single, as far as I knew.

Then there was the card he sent me after he visited me in New York in 1992, when I was in law school. He'd been in and out of a couple of colleges by then. We took a trip around Central Park in a carriage. I didn't want to think about that right now.

I looked at the last one, the one he sent me when Dad disappeared. It had his new phone number on it; new as of five years ago. And it was still his number the last time I saw him, in the summer of 1996. There was a quickening between my legs as I remembered that.

In July 1996 I went back home to Zanesville to help my mother move out of our house. I was between deals at Winslow. I'd just come back from three weeks in Italy, but I hadn't taken a vacation in over two years and the office told me I could relax. There was a window of opportunity, and the need was there. If I wanted to exercise any control on what my mother threw out, I had to be on the premises.

So I flew to Columbus, rented a car, and drove east on the interstate until I reached my hometown. I hadn't been there since '93, when my dad's trial was going on. None of us had shown up at the trial. Since the messy divorce in 1990, we'd maintained radio silence. There was another woman. My sisters and I rallied around our mother. I wanted to break ranks, but I didn't. I hadn't seen my father since that day in Philadelphia, on Locust Walk, when he told Caroline and me that he was leaving.

My old room was neat, for once. I've always been a total mess, all my life. Without my mother or a maid, I'm hopeless. Mom had cleaned it, and my stuff was laid out in categories, ready for my inspection, evaluation, and review.

"Be ruthless," she told me. "Nothing goes to Cincinnati. If you want it, you have to find a place for it in New York."

She wasn't, in the end, quite that strict, but I had to do some serious culling. Caroline and Pamela were there, too, going through the same drill. We ended up sitting around the kitchen table, looking at pictures. It was like the Soviet encyclopedia: there was the history of our family, but with Dad cut out. All the pictures of him were gone. It was just we four women; there were no husbands, boyfriends, or children around. My sisters had come alone, as I always had, so for once I didn't feel like such a stray.

For a few minutes, anyway.

"So are you seeing anyone in New York?" That was Pamela. She had to ask.

"No one special."

It was at that moment the doorbell rang. Mother fluttered her hands, and in walked Drew Gillespie. Turned out he'd been helping my mother pack up the place. Oh, yes. They were good buddies. Still. Something about his Irish Catholicism rang bells with her. Or maybe it was his Irish eyes.

He'd brought beer. He sat with us as we looked at pictures, and I didn't need to say much to him because Caroline and Pamela were doing a fine job of sustaining the conversation. I did my best to ignore him. Those were the days of my Manhattan men, the Brit and the German and the associate at my law firm. I wasn't going to let Drew back in. Caroline, who used to turn up her nose at Drew, now seemed to find him positively inspiring. Maybe it was the antique car business he'd built up. He was actually making money.

"How's that Big Apple?" he asked me.

"Still there."

We looked at more pictures and drank more beer, and my mother and my sisters gradually and strategically excused themselves until Drew and I were left alone. I told him I had to go upstairs and go through my stuff and he said "Let me help" and about a half hour later I had found my first mandolin, the very cheap one I bought before the Lyon & Healy I found later, and I started picking out a tune, "Paddy on the Turnpike," actually, and Drew went out to his truck and retrieved his guitar and two songs later I was thinking about the summer of 1983, and the stars over the Rosedale mine, and the first time he unbuttoned my shirt and slid my jeans off after undoing my combat boots with their ridiculously long laces and he'd given me my first orgasm and now, thirteen years later, in 1996, I set my mandolin down and lay back on the bed I'd slept in since I was eight and let him unbutton my shirt again and slip off my jeans and there was no delay with my shoes because I had been wearing slides with no socks and I'd kicked them off as soon as he stood up to take off his own clothes.

There he was, the way he'd been that first night in the mine, his stomach still muscled, his eyes still locked onto mine with that single-mindedness that excluded the world and focused on me in a way that no one else has ever done. I think I was exotic to him then, back from a world he didn't know. But his hands were on me in an Ivy League way; the same knowing touch he brought to a minor seventh chord or a fuel injection adjustment turned my body into a keyboard.

And when I came the first time, it was as if I were hearing the music in my head from a place at the bottom of the sea. My ears filled with cotton, my room was gone, and he wasn't even in me yet. I looked at his face, looking back at me from between my legs, and I pulled him up to my face and tasted his sweat, and he was murmuring that phrase he would murmur, the secret one I can't tell, the one I first heard that night in the Rosedale mine, and he said it again as I guided him in.

Still, when it was all over, I said good-bye to him, the way I did in 1988 and 1992. That third time would be the charm, I thought. Now, at the end of the century in Washington, D.C., I wrote his phone number down on the back of one of my own business cards and slid it in my wallet.

It was midnight in Zanesville. I looked at Drew's number for a long time before I put the shoe box back in the closet and tried to go to sleep.

daylight blasted down the escalator from the upper world, causing me to reach for my sunglasses. It seemed much too bright to be seven-thirty in the morning. But it was seven-thirty, and I was meeting Valerie for bagels in Cleveland Park, right at the subway stop. Time was tight, because I was catching a nine o'clock train for New York.

Which reminded me, I needed some cash.

Manhattan has a way of sucking money out of your pockets; just a block's walk and you've spent four hundred dollars without being able to account for any of it. So I approached an automated teller, planning to withdraw the daily maximum.

I had competition. A Cleveland Park mommy, wearing a down vest and Birkenstocks, bore down on my ATM with her kid in tow. We were almost the same distance away, approaching from different angles, and I wouldn't be able to beat her to it unless I picked up my pace in an obvious and unseemly way. So I hung back a step and allowed her in first. Big mistake.

"Jeffrey, can you punch in the number?"

Jeffrey was about four years old, and his mother's estimate of his capabilities far exceeded his capacity to deliver.

"Good try, Jeffrey! I'm going to whisper to you again."

The comfortable margin I had allowed to reach my breakfast rendezvous was evaporating. I puffed out my cheeks, exhaled audibly, cleared my throat.

"Oh, look, Jeffrey, it's given back our card. Are you ready to try again?"

Jeffrey's blundering nubs pressed another random sequence of buttons. A line had formed behind me. Three people. In my mind a pack of feral Dobermans snarled out of Rock Creek Park and tore mother and child to pieces.

"Put your hand on mine, here, and we'll press the numbers together."

A white-haired woman stood directly behind me in line. She was old enough to recall civilized public decorum. When I looked back at her, she winked and shook her head.

"Good, Jeffrey. That's very good."

Mother and son paraded by the line, radiating smug entitlement. Jeffrey wore some kind of expensive outdoorsy duds ordered from Seattle or the Maine woods. A future captain of industry, no doubt. An eliminator of American jobs.

I drew out my money and rushed to the bagel shop. Valerie was already there, waiting at an outdoor table with her onion bagel, no cream cheese, and her mocha java.

"Sorry I'm late."

"You're the one in a rush."

"I'll be right back."

I wanted a poppy seed bagel, but I was worried about the seeds sticking in my teeth. I settled for the less dangerous sesame, and a large black coffee.

"So tell me about this horrible date," I said.

Valerie made an unhappy face. Valerie Bernstein, my classmate from Columbia Law. We weren't especially close at Columbia. For one thing, I slept with her boyfriend. Not that she knew. He was an asshole, anyway, and she was better off rid of him. He ended up in Nigeria with Bechtel.

"It was unspeakable," she said. Our proximity in D.C. had made us friends of convenience.

"Say it, anyway."

"You won't believe it."

"Probably not."

"He was that guy from the World Bank. You know."

"Oh, Jesus."

"We went to the Kennedy Center."

"That overblown Holiday Inn."

"Whatever."

"They should just give up and rent it out for boat shows and tractor pulls."

"We saw this lute concert, a tribute to Julian Bream."

"That's nice."

"Yeah, it was nice. I actually thought of you."

"I would have liked it."

"Anyway, we came back up here, and we were having drinks at Nanny O'Brien's, and suddenly he announces that he doesn't think we'll be seeing each other again. Can you believe that?"

"Like, who cares, right?"

"He says, get this. He says I'm not smart enough for him."

"Oh, you're kidding."

"He says, 'I don't think this relationship has a future. You're not smart enough for me.'"

"No first-date sex for that boy."

"Can you believe that?"

"That's unbelievable."

"That he would say that? On a first date?"

"What happened to just not calling?"

"He felt he had to insult me to my face."

"It's amazing what men think they deserve. The dumpiest, dreariest wet smack thinks he should come home to Sophie Marceau. What did you say?"

"I just got up and left."

"Good for you."

"But I couldn't sleep all night. I can't believe I let that ridiculous dipshit get to me."

"He is ridiculous. And he is a dipshit. I've seen him."

"I hate Washington."

"It fucking sucks."

"I hate my job, too."

"Well, on that front I have no complaints."

"I know. You really lucked out. I can't believe it. Rosalind Wilcox, house counsel."

"What's so unbelievable?"

"You know what I mean."

"No, what do you mean?"

"Rosalind."

"Well, shit. I finished ahead of you at Columbia."

"What does that have to do with anything?"

"And I did five years on Wall Street. What did you do?"

"Rosalind, I came here to complain, not to get puked on all over again."

"Sorry."

"Did you have a bad night?"

"I had a great night."

"Are you seeing somebody?"

"No."

That made her feel better. Why not lie and make someone feel better? Especially if you have to lie for other reasons, anyway. She could never know about me and Marshall. That secret would hold for only nanoseconds.

"Are you looking?"

"No."

"You don't have to look."

"No one does. It's like watching water boil. Look away for a while, and things will take care of themselves."

"You sound so wise, Rosalind."

"Look, forget this guy."

"I'd like to."

"I'll introduce you to somebody. Nice guy. Named Barry Weiss. He asked me out yesterday."

"So what's wrong with him?"

"Nothing. It's a principle thing. He's a business associate."

"A lawyer?"

"Don't get picky."

"I've got this thing for bankers right now."

"And look what that got you."

"A lawyer. I don't know."

"He's a banking lawyer. Sort of. He does project finance."

"Oh, all right."

"Great."

"What's his name?"

"Barry. Barry Weiss."

"Is he going to tell me I'm not smart enough?"

"I'm just going to introduce you. You're on your own after that."

"Okay."

I looked at my watch.

"You have to be going," she said.

"I do."

"Have a good trip."

"I'll try."

On the subway to Union Station I briefly considered the wisdom of what I'd done. Was she really right for Half-Smoke? Or vice versa? Did they deserve each other? I didn't know. I couldn't carry the weight of the whole world on my shoulders.

I was late and had to run down the platform to catch the Metroliner. The upside of being late was I didn't have to sit with Marshall and Lucius. The car was full! Too bad they didn't have smoking cars anymore. You used to always be able to get a seat among America's last nonconformists.

"I'll be in the next car," I said.

"Fine. We don't need to go over anything, do we?"

"I'm set if you are."

"We'll see you up there."

I was happy to be able to relax, but slightly disappointed that I wasn't more indispensable. You can't have it both ways,

I suppose. And I couldn't sit and flirt with Marshall, something that after an hour or so of riding I knew I was going to be in the mood to do.

So I sat with my papers and intermittently read a magazine. Outside the window, I could see the crumbling industrial backside of the northeast corridor; the distribution infrastructure you can only see from a train, the formstone-coated houses, the mudflat rivers sprinkled with tires. We passed freight trains, lines of boxcars pulled up on sidings. Southern served the South. They also gave a Green Light to Innovations. North of Baltimore, I pulled a folder out of my briefcase.

Here was the deal: a pipeline in Colombia. British Petroleum had a 35 percent stake in the project. They had a subsidiary corporation set up in Colombia, incorporated under Colombian laws, but the real owners were B.P. and Trans-Canada Pipe Lines. And there were a bunch of other partners—Fluor, some emerging market funds, and some private Colombian investment companies. And us. Rigel Associates. We had 3 percent of the deal. We were partnered with one of the private Colombian companies, plus we were running a pool of capital from our own investors. Offshore money. Some of that was also Colombian. And South African. We were very popular with South African investors. Lucius was always making pitches in Johannesburg and Cape Town. I'd gone with him a couple of times, but I hate Africa. I'm spoiled, I admit it.

"Philadelphia," the conductor said.

I thought of Thirtieth Street Station, the beautiful concourse with the statue of the Buggering Angel. The first time Marshall ever kissed me was under that statue. It took him nearly three months to get around to making a move. I thought for a while I was going to have to do everything myself.

I put away the Colombian file and opened the South African one. This was the headache of the day, leaving aside the Swiss escrow account. The empty escrow account. This was our diamond mine. The diamond mine, and the associated power plant providing the electricity to run the hole. We had an unusual arrangement here. Rigel Associates had money in both the mine and the power plant. The vehicle was a holding company, incorporated in the Cayman Islands, called Xantex. The power financing was linked to the mine, since the mine was the main customer for the power. That was the project finance angle.

Project finance. That's what we call it when a loan is paid off by the revenues of the project in question. Say it's a power plant. In a third world country, maybe, or maybe not. A bunch of American banks and American investors put up money to build the plant, and what they're offered in return is a share of the income when the completed plant starts selling electricity. Maybe the World Bank shores things up and issues whispered reassurances. Or maybe not. Anyway, that was the business we were in.

In this case the South African government was guaranteeing the bonds financing the plant construction. But the projected revenue stream depended on the mine. And South Africa, of course, wasn't what it used to be. From the standpoint of our Xantex clients, that wasn't necessarily something to cheer. In college I went to "Free South Africa" demonstrations, circa 1985; now I wondered what kind of underwriting guarantee I could get out of the African National Congress government. Anything could go wrong. And what good were the protective covenants in a New York–drafted contract when the winds of chaos really blew down across the veldt?

Not my problem, really. As long as the covenants are there, I've done my job. Too bad paper can't stop bullets or poisoned arrows.

I looked at clause 7a, as redrafted by Half-Smoke. He was going to bill us three hours for this one paragraph of bad prose, at better than $365 an hour once his junior associate's time was rolled in. And I was paying over $250 an hour for his sorry ass alone. It was ridiculous. I could have done it myself in fifteen minutes. But Marshall and Lucius liked the big-firm involvement, useless and overpriced as it was. They themselves were under no illusions about the worth of law firm work, but our clients were very reassured. That was what we were paying for. Balm for the nervous client.

The new proposed reimbursement rate for a force majeure power interruption was 25 percent. Just as I'd requested. I'd handed copies of this new draft to Lucius and Marshall, but of course they weren't bothering to look at it. I figured Lucius might make a scene when he found out I didn't do what he told me to do. But if I did everything he told me, I wouldn't be a counselor.

We passed my favorite sight on the trip: the bridge over the Delaware with the sign TRENTON MAKES, THE WORLD TAKES. Neither clause was true anymore, but it was a nice thought. A benchmark in the decline of the empire. When that sign appeared, we were on our way up. Now we're on our way down.

My first glimpse of the World Trade Center took me back to my first trip to New York, in August of '89, when I rode the train north after visiting my sister at Penn. I was starting law school. Caroline was in medical school, following in our father's footsteps, except that she was doing it in the Ivy League instead of at the Buckeye state institution. We never asked ourselves where the money was coming from, to send her to Mount Holyoke and me to Kenyon, Patricia to Cornell, the twins to Barnard and Yale. Quite a track record, five girls and half a million dollars' worth of sheepskin. I might have gone out of state with the rest of them except that I spent too much time in strip mines with Drew Gillespie and too many other boys. After a year in a D.C. group house, though, I decided to get with the program. Law school. New York City. And one last money transfusion from dear old Dad. I never stopped to add it up, how a small-town G.P. with a stay-at-home wife sent five kids to top-drawer colleges, and the three youngest to private high school as well. What did I know? I was in the ninth grade before I found out his real name wasn't Wilcox. And I had left home before I saw the neighborhood in Pittsburgh where he'd grown up. Squalid is a kind way to describe it. He and Andy Warhol were born on the very same street. Did Dad ever tell me that? No way.

So I rode the train up that day in '89. I'd come from D.C. to Philadelphia for a stopover. When I saw the Lower Manhattan skyline, the twin butter sticks of the World Trade Center, I felt what every provincial arrival feels: that I was finally coming home. I didn't imagine I'd end up dreading the sight of those towers, dreading the ride to the forty-eighth floor of the Triangle Trust Building, hating my view of Governors Island, hating my even better view of all of Manhattan stretched out to the north; I was a helpless sardine in that glittering net of lights: a deadline-imprisoned junior associate.

And now we were under the Hudson, and I knew the drill: the brief light-well view of the old New Yorker hotel, the rocking screech of the slowing train; then out into the ghastly subterranean waste of Penn Station; the taxi ride down Seventh Avenue with me wedged between the two men, our thighs in electric contact, our mouths rapping about spreads and yields and ratings and basis points. Finally the dump-out on Liberty Street, the scene of my dream, my midnight execution. Then the ride heavenward, Marshall gingerly lifting his feet, the tender legacy of last night's fun. And the elevator doors opening on the forty-eighth floor, the three of us crossing to the reception desk like a rifle squad taking a hill.

"We're here to see Eric Hoffman."

"He's expecting you."

Indeed he was. He came out to the lobby to greet us. Accompanying him was another embarrassment for me: Jay Hixon, former lover and professional sad sack. Let me explain. During my time at Winslow, I became the object of Eric Hoffman's—Super Wiener's—intense sexual interest. No big deal, except that he was married and my boss. And there was, ultimately, an ugly scene. A proposition, properly refused by me. In the very office, in fact, where the five of us were now sitting, making preliminary chitchat. Nice view of Governors Island, and in the far distance, the Verrazano Narrows. Oh, I'd known what was on the Wiener's mind, how he saw it all playing out: an Italian restaurant in the East Village, maybe, after he'd driven over from Englewood Cliffs and had the Lexus safely garaged, and over a long dinner and drinks things would just fall into place. But it didn't happen. He never saw the inside of my apartment. And I made a point of taking up with Hixon, first-year nobody Hixon, Hixon who looked like he just fell off his skateboard, never-to-be-partner Hixon. Oh, that tore the Wiener up. Good-looking Wiener, Wiener whose partner draw last year was $832,000, including the $90,000 premium from that California utility deal. At this meeting it was obvious that he was still not over it. He was staring at Hixon, pondering. And who could blame him? Seldom has the fundamental inequity of God-given physiognomy been so graphically displayed. But tough shit, Mr. Wiener. Sometimes the losers win.

But not for long. And that's why I was embarrassed. Jay Boy was giving me the hangdog look. The "Why did you do it?" look. He seems to have forgotten that he was more interested in my shoes than he was in me. Instead of counting his blessings and cherishing the memory of his ephemeral good fortune, he was pouting. And losing my sympathy.

"Rosalind?"

That was Lucius, whispering in my ear. He'd finally glanced at the redrafted clause 7a. He may have wanted to shout at me, but we were in a meeting. We had to show a united front.

"I gave you a copy of that," I whispered. "What did you do on the ride up? Talk about Switzerland?"

"A bit. All right, I'll trust you on this. But only so far."

Marshall was asking for a briefing on the British Petroleum agreement. We were seeing them next. Or their lawyers, anyway. Same building, ten floors up. Super Wiener gave his spiel. I couldn't help myself. I had to interrupt.

"Look. I know Colombia is a criminal racket disguised as a country, but they have environmental laws. They have a Ministry of the Environment, in fact, and I saw no acknowledgment of that in the draft. We've got a payment risk there, if there are any changes in Colombian environmental laws after the bid date."

"That's a good point," the Wiener said. "Jay, let's look at that."

I was feeling good. I had the whip out.

"Let's put in a tariff adjustment, allowing for greater or lesser cost to the carrier if there are any, blah-blah, aforementioned changes in environmental laws, blah-blah, or changes in the specifications for environmental mitigation that the parties have already agreed on."

They were all looking at me. Four men, at my mercy.

"And force majeure. We're nowhere near where we need to be. Colombia is full of terrorists, as I'm sure you've noticed. Not everybody is excited about our pipeline and the wonderful foreign investment it represents. Is there anything in that draft about guerrilla terrorist attacks on the pipeline? Not that I could find."

"She's really onto this terrorist thing," Lucius said, smiling at the Wiener.

"Well, she should be," Marshall said. Good boy.

"Rights-of-way," I said. "Are we covered there?"

"What's the problem?" asked Marshall.

"You don't have one hundred percent of the rights-of-way you need to complete this project," Super Wiener said.

"That's a problem for the lead underwriter and the Colombian government," said Marshall.

"Yes, but you want to be protected," said Super Wiener.

"That's right," I said.

"We're putting in a clause obligating the Colombians to indemnify your investors for certain standby costs and for payment of scheduled principal and interest on the financing if the rights-of-way are not obtained in a timely fashion and result in a construction delay."

"That sounds good," Lucius said.

"Rosalind?" Marshall nodded at me.

"Seems to cover it," I said.

"Great," said Marshall. "Now, how about the Xantex contract?"

Africa time. Nobody looked comfortable. Super Wiener buzzed his partner, Wallace Farrell, aka K.A. We, the clients, then watched three overpaid Paul Stuart mannequins take turns reading aloud to us the same material we held in our hands. That's corporate law. Nice work if you can get it.

"Rosalind?" Marshall, again.

"I guess," I said. "For now, anyway."

"Sounds good," Lucius said. "Thank you all. Rosalind will be in touch."

I shook hands with my former employers, now entirely under my thumb. There was none of the inappropriate physical contact I used to experience constantly. No hugs, pecks, or pinches. They were models of professional rectitude.

"Be afraid," I told them, from the door, out of Marshall's and Lucius's hearing. "Be very afraid."

feeling boho, we had our postmortem dinner at an Italian place in the Village. People who managed to live without working traipsed by on Bleecker Street. I remembered that life, all cigarettes and shared rooms.
"Well, that wasn't so bad," Lucius said.
"Says you." That was *moi*. With a mouthful of linguini.
"I thought it was productive," Marshall said.

"Why don't we go ahead and get a bottle of wine?" Me again. Thirsty now.

Marshall ordered the wine. Lucius told a story about an earlier encounter with K.A., how he pitched the firm's services on a long-ago deal only to get pinched off when the investing partners consolidated their legal representation.

"He said he felt like Pete Best," Lucius said.

"Pete Best?" I asked. Big mistake. So I know now: he was the Beatles' first drummer. The Beatles! I had to listen to that sort of shit all the time with those two.

"I was at their first American concert," Lucius said.

"You were? Really."

"My dad was stationed at Bolling. I was in high school. In Arlington. And I was there, at the Washington Coliseum. Their first show, 1964."

"Yeah, well," I said. "My mother wore bobby socks and once saw Frank Sinatra."

"No, Rosalind," Lucius said. "It was an historic event."

"Oh, come on."

"And you should see the Coliseum now."

"Where is it?"

"Northeast. Up by the rail yards, north of Union Station. It's just an industrial facility now. A trash transfer station."

"It's a garbage dump? That's funny."

"It's not funny. It's hallowed ground."

"Nineteen sixty-four. I was still at Annapolis." This was Marshall. "Eventually I'd be on my way to the South China Sea." He was full of a different kind of nostalgia. The New Frontier. Allen Dulles. The front line of the Cold War. I didn't know how much of this I was going to be able to take. But I knew where it was going. The grand convergence.

These two guys, the ex-navy spook and the Columbia draft dodger, were thinking about Kennedy. I could see it in their eyes: the slight shift, the faint disconnect that seemed to prevent people their age from looking at the simple truth of the assassination: one boring kook really did kill the dream, and he did it all by himself.

"Ask me where I was when Kennedy was shot," I said.

I have such a great answer to that question: I wasn't even born.

but I did have a coincidental connection to the Kennedy assassination: my date and time of birth.

"That's right. November 22, 1966. Approximately 2:10 P.M. eastern time. My mother went into labor about four in the morning, started seriously pushing around one-thirty, and by the time I came out, the president had been dead three years to the minute."

Marshall and I were in bed, in the Gramercy Park Hotel.

Part of the boho thing we had going. After that bottle of wine and all.

"So you've got just over a shopping month until my thirty-third birthday."

"I'll try not to disappoint you."

I kissed him, wanting him to feel better. We'd gone through an elaborate pantomime to get here; I'd walked south from Bleecker down into SoHo, explaining that I was going to visit a friend, while Marshall and Lucius went uptown to the Regency, where they both had rooms. But Marshall had grabbed a taxi on Lexington Avenue, I had jumped into one on Lafayette, and finally we were all over each other in an elevator at the Gramercy. But our flop into the sack was a little disappointing. I was detached, for some reason. I found myself looking at the room fixtures, the wall moldings. His little grunts in my ear began to irritate me. I was conscious of the stubble on his jaw, of the potential for pain in the morning.

Marshall, of course, felt my distance. I didn't want it that way, but I could see myself through his eyes. Periodically I noted his awareness emerging from the cloud of his own exertions to focus on my face, and I knew what he was seeing: my slack lips tightening slightly into a smile that teetered between encouragement and derision, and my open eyes, watching him as they would watch any spectacle that threatened to turn boring. Evaluating, skeptical, forbearing. I don't think he actually finished. He gave up and rolled off me. And now I was engaged in damage control.

"So where were you, darling?"

"Hmm?"

"When you heard that Kennedy was shot."

Marshall pressed his palms to his face, massaging his forehead with his fingertips.

"I was coming out of an English class at the Naval Academy," he said. "It was my second year there. I remember I'd just learned to find Diego Garcia on a map."

"Where is that?"

"In the middle of the Indian Ocean."

"Fun."

"Yeah, well. I ended up there a few years later."

"What did you think when you heard the news?"

"About the assassination?"

"Did you think it was a coup?"

"I thought it was the Cubans. Acting for the Russians."

"What do you think now?"

"I don't know."

I kissed a ring around his navel, feeling the soft accumulation of fat, thinking of a particular Mediterranean boy and his sharply incised abdomen.

"Well, you were an intelligence officer. And a contract spook. Right?"

"I suppose."

"So did you ever hear anything?"

"Not really. No."

I licked his chest. All over. I was going to turn this thing around.

"I remember in 1967," Marshall said. "Summer of Love."

"Yes?"

"I remember thinking about the year 2000 and how old I'd be."

"Well, here you are. You're still alive."

"What are we going to do for New Year's Eve?"

"Whatever you want."
"Let's just be alone."
"Okay."
"No faxes, no phones."
"You're the boss."
"No, you are."
"Whatever." I gave him a light slap.
"I missed all that, you know."
"All what?"
"Summer of Love. All of that."
"That was all bullshit, anyway."
"I was out of it. Laos. Five years."
"I think you liked it there."
"Where?"
"Laos."

He ran his hand through my hair as I headed south. He was erect again. I wasn't feeling detached anymore.

"I want to take you there someday," he murmured.
"Me. To Laos."
"Yes."
"It's a nice place?"
"We fucked it up. We destroyed it."
"Are you sorry?"
"I'm very sorry."

I took him in my mouth and did my thing. And I'm sure it was never better for him, not even in Vientiane.

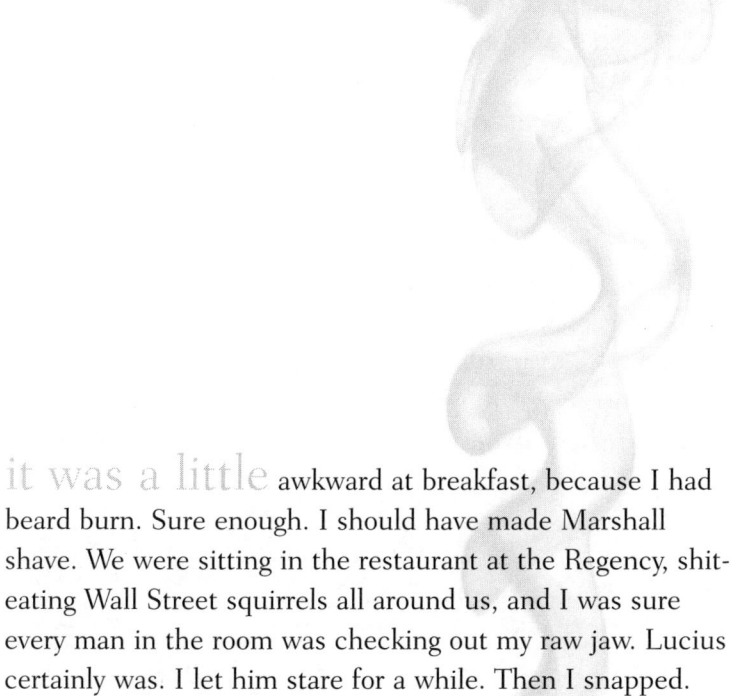

it was a little awkward at breakfast, because I had beard burn. Sure enough. I should have made Marshall shave. We were sitting in the restaurant at the Regency, shit-eating Wall Street squirrels all around us, and I was sure every man in the room was checking out my raw jaw. Lucius certainly was. I let him stare for a while. Then I snapped.

"An old friend, all right?"

"I guess so."

"So eat your eggs and shut up."

"Touchy."

I was wearing my most expensive suit, which only served to call extra attention to my blazing chin. Marshall was worrying a grapefruit. He was the only one who hadn't looked at me.

"See," I said. "Look at Marshall. He knows it's not his business. Discretion. I like that in a man."

Why couldn't I restrain myself around Lucius? I didn't even like the guy.

"They're not discreet down in SoHo. And they don't shave, evidently."

I leaned close to him for my statutory "Fuck you."

The waiter elegantly refilled my coffee. I'd been a good girl, ordering only fruit and an English muffin. And now I was starving. I wanted to go to Roy Rogers. There weren't any on Park Avenue, I didn't think. Two sausage and egg biscuits would have been about right.

"Here comes our boy."

"I'll introduce you, Rosalind."

"So this is him."

It was. Roos Van Zyk. I'd never seen him in the flesh before. He was big. A roughneck. A man on the business end of things, where all our abstract contract talk was translated into South African slave labor.

"Roos!" That was Lucius.

"Atkinson, you pooftah," the man said. That set off another bell for me. I had wondered, idly, if Lucius was gay. He'd been married, long ago, but didn't seem very busy these days. For a man with millions, he didn't go on many dates.

"Roos, this is our attorney, Rosalind Wilcox."

I took his hand, watching the rough corners of his mouth

curl up as he registered my facial burn. It was a bad moment. But who hasn't been a fool for love, one time or another?

"I've heard so much about you," Van Zyk said. What was that supposed to mean? His mouth flattened out, but the insinuations were still there, in his blue eyes. He was a Boer farmer, or came from Boer farmer stock. His tie was askew, and though his suit was first quality, it seemed too small on him, too wrinkled—he looked as if he'd run from the barnyard, had a quick shower, then hopped on a mule for the ride to East Sixty-first Street.

"I'm a little worried," he said. "You guys are sitting farther from the windows than you used to."

"We got here late," Lucius said, looking at me.

"Don't look at me," I said.

"I'm just a little worried," Van Zyk said again.

"Don't be," said Marshall. "We ran this deal by the outside counsel again this morning, and I think things are coming together."

"What do you think?" Van Zyk was looking at me. "Rosalind, is it?"

"Yes. And aside from some terrorism covenants, I don't think there are problems."

"Yes. Terrorism." He slathered butter on a muffin in a way that made me think of some of my rural uncles. "I don't like that business about the terrorism."

"It's a real issue," I said. I wanted a cigarette. Bad.

"Not really," Van Zyk said. "No. Marshall, should we enlighten counsel?"

"Counsel knows what she's talking about."

"All right." Van Zyk worked on his muffin. "I see how it is."

"How is it?" That was me.

"We'll do it your way," Van Zyk said. "We'll sign the thing, force majeure provisions and all."

What was this? They'd all been talking! Behind my back! Working it all out. What the fuck was this?

"Wait a minute. Did I miss something?"

"No," Lucius said. "I faxed him your draft last night. You didn't seem to be in your hotel room."

"All right. We'll leave it at that."

There I was, at breakfast at the Regency. Discussing business. For my presence I was paid $158,000 a year, less than the $170,000 I was making at Winslow, but still a sweet salary for Washington, D.C. And for an easier job. I looked around the room, at the power people mumbling to each other and gassing into their cell phones. What a scene. I had to contrast it with my arrival in New York, ten years before. That dorm room on the sixth floor of Johnson Hall, where I'd look out over Harlem and put off opening my lawbooks. Flirting with the mailman, Frank, who used to write "cutie pie" and "sweetie pie" on all the girls' mail, until a coffle of harpies complained. Toxic waste from the feminist hothouse. And later, my hovel of an apartment on 108th Street, the sort of hole you're grateful to land in once you've adopted Manhattan standards. The same hovel I loafed through another year in while acquiring an LL.M. Then my job offer at Winslow, Cooper—they were paying first-years $83,000. That's the most anyone ever made for knowing nothing. Up to then, anyway. It's six figures now. What do you know after law school, after three years of bias awareness seminars and deconstructing oppressive hierarchies? Nothing. Jack shit. Eighty-three thousand looks good. So I moved downtown a ways, first to West Seventy-sixth Street, then down to

Chelsea. Ate all my meals at the Empire Diner. And now I was at the Regency. At a power breakfast in my power suit. Too bad about the beard burn.

"By the way," I said, "have we figured out the problem with the Swiss account?"

They all happened to have their mouths full. They just looked at me, like cows chewing their cuds.

"I mean, it's something we need to resolve, don't you think?"

"Rosalind." That was Van Zyk. "Are you free this evening?"

it's a testament to the power of the client that Marshall just let Van Zyk take me away for the rest of the day. The beard burn put me at a disadvantage, since the South African read me—not entirely inaccurately—as a loose woman, and decided—not entirely inaccurately—that there was an attraction between us. Like every other man I ever met, he couldn't resist lecturing me. I must look like I want to learn something. Today, evidently, we were going to begin with Charles de Gaulle.

"Are you familiar with his memoirs?"

"I didn't know he wrote his memoirs."

"He begins his war memoirs by comparing his country to a princess or a Madonna."

"Typical frog."

"De Gaulle always thought of France as a woman."

I did my best to stifle a yawn.

"As investment bankers, we could learn from de Gaulle."

"Well, I'm not actually a banker, you know."

"I know. But de Gaulle didn't share our romance with credit."

"No?"

"No. And your country has never forgiven France for not signing on to your game in the sixties."

Oh, no. Not the goddamn sixties.

"De Gaulle kept saying, 'Show me ze gold.'" It was funny, hearing his Afrikaner accent imitating French. "Of course, you didn't have it to show."

"Credit makes the world go round. And getting rid of gold was the best thing we ever did."

"We'll see."

I'd fought off the craving for a cigarette all day, but I was at the end of my rope. We were outside, sitting under the Cinzano umbrellas at a generic Columbus Avenue eatery. I don't know why we were there. You know how it is in New York—you have an array of the best restaurants in the world, and you end up under the bullshit Cinzano umbrellas, eating some bullshit sandwich.

"You mind if I smoke?"

"Not at all."

They never do, it seems. Not when it's me doing the asking. I took out my Export As, and he reached across the table to give me a light. He was equipped. Some fancy Deco-style butane job.

"Thank you."

"You're welcome."

"Tell me something."

"My pleasure."

"What's going on? With Xantex."

His eyes narrowed, a little piggishly; it was an expression he might use in sizing up a stray from Soweto found loitering on the back forty.

"Nothing's going on. Everything's on track."

"Four million dollars disappeared."

"Your bosses didn't mention that."

"You know what I'm talking about, don't you?"

"I don't keep up with internal accounting."

"You might notice four million bucks."

"And I might not. This is a two-hundred-million-dollar deal."

"With problems."

"Americans don't understand Africa."

"Maybe you don't understand Americans."

"Americans think they can babyproof the world. They think life is a Disney movie."

"We're a childish people. I'll grant you that."

"Hard times are coming. Hard times that will call for hard choices."

"Don't tell that to Wall Street."

"Listen to me. I hate Marxism. I hate communists. No one hates them more than me. But I know something. Marx isn't dead. You think he's dead. You talk about the end of history—"

"I don't talk about any such thing."

"—but Marx will have the last laugh. He was just a century off, that's all. The contradictions are piling up. And what always happens? A world war, to shake out the contradictions. That's what World War I did, and it took World War II to settle the hierarchy. You had to apply nuclear persuasion to the Japanese. That's all breaking down now. And what are you going to do this time around? Who's going to fight for you? You'll have to get all your killers out of prison or therapy or wherever you've stashed them. You'll have to pray your hired Hessians will hold the line for you. But it won't happen. You'll lose."

I'm drawn to men with convictions, even when I know they're full of shit. I blew smoke rings, which only encouraged him.

"There's not enough pie to go around," he said. "Two reasons: world markets can't absorb future production, and future production is going to bring on an environmental catastrophe. And we get this end-of-history happy talk . . ."

"I told you. Not from me."

"When the U.S. goes the way of Britain, which will happen within the next fifty years, and probably sooner, you won't go quietly. You have bombs, and you're going to drop them. Too bad you're selling them to everybody else. That's what's going to make it a world war. You've leveled the playing field."

"Has anyone ever told you how boring you are, Roos?"

"The end of the British Empire was clouded in the rise of the American one. They handed the world off to you like an American football. But the next time around it's going to be like a fumble, and there are going to be all these huge players jumping for the loose ball."

"I would have pegged you as a rugby player."

"I like American football."

"Hmm."

"Rugby, too. So: all these depression predictors—they're right, but the timeline is too short. It's not going to happen yet. It's not going to happen until more of Asia comes up online and the U.S. can't afford to buy their surplus production anymore. Then we'll have the big old depression. We had the Great Depression? This will be the Greater Depression. And we'll solve it the same way we solved the last one. With a world war."

"Do I have to kiss you to shut you up?"

"That might work."

I blew out a protective smoke cloud. He was a self-made man, like my father. An asshole, yet I wanted his approval. I'm sure a therapist would have some glib advice for me—but on the ground, in the electric aura of irrational attraction, therapeutic good advice is irrelevant.

"What is your point here?"

"My point is that Africa's day will come. Now is the time to invest in Africa. Now when no one can see any hope."

"Noted."

I looked into his blue eyes and saw something hard there. Something I first saw in my father's eyes when I was about ten and showing him the first essay I'd ever written for school. He wasn't impressed. "You've got a lot to learn," he told me. I cried for days.

claudia, seeing the remnants of my beard burn, hid her smile behind her hands.

"How was your trip?" she asked.
"I'll tell you about it at lunch."
"How about the Green Beard?"
"Very funny."

But that's where we ended up. The Green Beard was an Irish dive over by Union Station. We walked from the office, through the October leaves of the park north of the Capitol. I told Claudia about meeting the client. Van Zyk.

"Did he . . . ?"

"No. No, no, no, no, no."

"Who, then?"

"Some guy."

"Some guy?"

"Some guy I used to know in New York."

I didn't want to be lying to her, but I couldn't let on about Marshall. Not yet. I hadn't told *anybody,* which was an amazing accomplishment. One of the greatest feats of my life up to then.

"From law school?"

"Well, that's when I met him. He's not a lawyer."

Our waiter at the Green Beard was named O'Shaughnessy. He was in his sixties, a refugee from Boston who'd washed up on Capitol Hill. We always sat at the same table in his area, resigned to slow service.

"God *damn* it, ladies, we got slammed! I'll be with you when I can."

"No problem, Mr. Shaughn."

O'Shaughnessy considered himself "slammed" if he had more than two tables to handle at once. The place was no more than a third full and, except for O'Shaughnessy himself, appeared placid.

"So tell me about this Van Zyk."

"Have you met him?"

"No. Talked to him on the phone."

"Real redneck. South African variety."

"I think he's a little scary."

"Really."

"Don't you?"

"I don't know."

"You like him, don't you?"

"What are you talking about?"

"I can tell. Look at you. Are you sure you didn't—"

"Shut up. He's an arrogant racist bore. No."

O'Shaughnessy came to the table and launched into a tirade about the Redskins. He remembered when they were in Boston, he said. Claudia fielded the football talk. She wasn't bad at it. All those nights in sports bars, sparring with the hammerheads.

"Can we order, Shaughnie?"

He flounced his apron and looked at me with exaggerated attention, his eyebrows raised. He stroked his chin.

"What happened to you?"

"Let's not discuss it. Can we order?"

"Why, yes, my lovely. What will you be having?"

"Chili nachos."

"You want to die young, don't you?" That was Claudia.

"I do. The younger, the better."

"Your arteries must look like cheese cannoli."

That remark made me so anxious I augmented my order with a load of fried mozzarella sticks.

"You sick puppy," said Claudia when Mr. O'Shaughnessy had toddled off toward the kitchen.

"I'm self-medicating."

"Is that it?"

"Well, you help me eat them."

"I won't."

"Yes, you will. Watch."

And of course she did. She told me about a date she had, trying, I think, to draw me out about my time in New York. She went to a poetry reading at the Library of Congress.

"It was okay."

As a choice of leisure time activity, I rank poetry readings just ahead of listening to Tammy Faye Bakker sing "Over the Rainbow." But I was civil. "Was he cute?"

"Sort of. I liked his glasses. So how about your guy?"

"He's good-looking."

"How so?"

"You've seen him." Uh-oh. It was coming. I was going to spill the beans.

"I've seen him? Where?"

"At work."

"Oh, my God."

I shrugged.

"Marshall. Oh, my God."

"Shhhhh."

We leaned toward each other. We were practically nose-to-nose.

"You have to keep this a secret."

"Oh, my God."

"You have to. Promise."

"I promise. How long has this . . . ?"

"A year."

"A *year*!"

We rocked upright again. O'Shaughnessy was headed our way.

"How's your love life, Mr. Shaughn?" I asked.

He did some kind of obscene pantomime, shaking his hips and pumping his fists.

"Boom boom *boom!*" he said.

That was a load of shit, but I laughed and winked at him. I admired his spunk. I love seeing a loser soldier on.

"You da man, Shaughnie," Claudia said.

"When I die, they'll have to knock it down with a baseball bat," he said.

I watched his weary back as he walked away toward the kitchen. I was thinking: death may not be far off for you. Boom boom boom.

"Well, speaking of Marshall," said Claudia.

"What?"

"I got a very interesting phone call."

"Really."

"From the FBI."

"The FBI?"

"They want to speak to Marshall."

"What about?"

"I have no idea."

"When was this?"

"Day before yesterday."

"Hmmm."

"Has he talked to them yet?"

"No idea."

"He didn't mention this to me."

"He's probably busy. It's probably nothing."

"You think?"

"I don't know."

"What would the FBI want with Marshall?"

Claudia looked at me over the top of her iced tea.

"You tell me," she said.

back at the office, I had to face the worst part of my job: actual work. While I was scampering around New York, papers were piling up in my in-box. We had a bunch of new deal possibilities. Money was sloshing around the world, looking for a place to rest. I had contracts, terms sheets, prospectuses, credit agreements. And a pain in my temples. I had to vet the stuff and assign it around to our outside counsel. Then I had to look at what the outside counsel sent back.

Questions, reservations. Marginal notations. I hate marginal notations. But I made a lot of them. By sundown, I had a long list of contract omissions, my work for the day: refine actual cost estimate, specify fee rate . . . gross negligence? . . . inadequate description of lump sum calculations . . . reimbursement indenture . . . incentives, penalties, key dates, question of design responsibility . . . fitness for purpose, subordinate debt holders' recourse . . . liability of subcontractors on procurement items . . . question of warranties and assignment thereof . . . questions of price and price fluctuation . . . insurance assignments . . . joint and several liability . . . completion tests . . . retentions and bonding.

And so on. No wonder I had a headache. I leaned back in my chair and looked at the ceiling.

Van Zyk. His blue eyes.

The characters on my computer screen went in and out of focus. Instead of paragraphs of legalese, I heard Van Zyk murmuring in my ear. I shook my head to clear the fuzz.

I had before me a credit agreement concerning a power plant in Venezuela. I was reviewing a contingency clause covering the delivery of the turbines. The Venezuelan government wanted to be assured that currency exchange rate fluctuations would not raise their costs above a certain threshold. The turbines were manufactured in Britain; if the bolivar fell against the pound, costs could rise unacceptably. The lead underwriter had worked out an agreement whereby the rate of payment was tied to the exchange rate. If the pound went up, the Brits got their money at a slower rate. If it went down, they got it faster. Within limits. Within relatively narrow parameters. If things swung more wildly, there would be a renegotiation. For the outside counsel, the time spent was billable either way.

Exchange rate up, rate of payment down. Those concepts had to compete with Marshall and Van Zyk for my available brain space. Van Zyk was winning. What was wrong with me? I thought of the South African's hands, his big wrists emerging from his shirt cuff. The fine hairs on the first joint of his fingers. He was wearing a wedding band, a thick gold thing. Gold was big where he came from.

"Excusa me."

It was the cleaning woman, a Latina who spoke almost no English. Every night she came through, emptied the trash, and apologized about the vacuum noise.

"No, no problem."

She smiled shyly, flashing gold teeth. I'm some kind of shaman to her, I thought. I put on a wool suit and I'm paid tens of thousands of dollars. For what? For nothing. She sees me here, night after night, moving papers, an alchemist.

"Look here," I said to her. "It's all about exchange rates. And bonds."

"Lo siento."

"No, no, listen. The bonds must be L.C.-backed."

"I am sorry."

"Don't be. If the rating agencies are unkind, the underwriters will be stuck with a load of shitpaper that nobody will buy."

"I am sorry. I will no vacuum."

"The Venezuelans will have to pay exorbitant interest. The markets will smell blood. The whole deal could unravel. You see?"

She didn't. She was from Guatemala, where her whole family had been butchered in the civil war. I imagined a chicken rhythmically poking its head out the doorless entry of a corrugated metal shack and disappearing back inside as if it were on an oval track traversing the dirt floor. You'd think I would count my blessings, be content with my good fortune, forget the throb in my cranium. You'd think that.

You'd be wrong.

I called up the Xantex contract. As long as I was thinking of Van Zyk, I might as well focus on his business. So he'd signed it, force majeure provisions and all. I scrolled down the document, looking for problems. I came to the section dealing with completion bond money. How it was to go into an escrow account.

That was the missing money. The $4 million gone from that Swiss bank in Chiasso.

It was after nine. I was alone in the office. This might be a good time to look around, I thought.

I wandered upstairs. I parked myself at Lucius's desk and signed on to his computer. We all had shared files, but I was hoping something different might turn up. A Xantex file. One I didn't have. One the police might want to see.

I called up the accounts and scrolled down through them. Aeolus Power. British Petroleum. Cryolon AFC International. Paracelsus Partners, Ltd. Xantex. There were subfiles under Xantex. They were locked, but I could read the titles. Executive Resources. I'd heard that name, had seen disbursements, but I wasn't sure who that was. Quilty Equity Partners. News to me. The Augustine Group.

Augustine Group.

It wouldn't open, kept asking me for a special password.

FUCK, I typed. No go.

Augustine. That was the name my father used for his sham real estate company. It had to be a coincidence.

I stared at the screen, my vision blurring again.

When Drew visited me in New York in 1992, while we

were riding around the park in the horse-drawn carriage, while he was putting his hands all over me and I wasn't responding because this was New York and this was the new me and I hadn't been amused by his country-boy caterwauling of an ancient Charlie Daniels song, "Still in Saigon," and his pretending to gawk at the high buildings, while I put his hand back in his own lap and pointed out the Dakota to him, he asked me a funny question.

"Did you know your dad has a Swiss bank account?"

This was right after Dad was arrested the first time, but two years before he skipped bail and disappeared. And the answer was no, I hadn't heard about any Swiss account. And I got mad at Drew for reminding me of certain things, and for taking such an interest in my family in general, and my dad in particular.

I got so mad at him.

Now I took out my business card with Drew's phone number on it. I wondered if he would be home. Or alone. Then I wondered if I should dial the number from an office phone; it would show up on the bill, and Lucius might notice it. Would he really? I couldn't know. The guy, I realized, might be monitoring everything.

Augustine.

That was really weird. So weird that I ended up dialing Drew's number. A machine came on. Everyone had a machine. Even in Zanesville. I could probably e-mail him, if I knew the address.

"Drew, honey," I said, "it's me. Rosalind. I know it's been a while, and I was wondering how you're doing. Call me." I gave him the number. "Or come see me. I want to ask you something about my dad. Talk to you soon, I hope."

Oh, why did I say that? *Come see me.* It just popped out. I wanted to slap myself.

At eleven I sat down at my own desk again. I deleted a month's worth of junk e-mail. I wrote a letter to White & Case, giving them shit about their bill. I wrote another to the IRS, growling and posturing. Doing my Xena thing. Another escrow issue, that was. Then a fax to Covington & Burling. Another fax, to Sumitomo Bank in San Francisco. Then an e-mail instruction to Claudia: a list of things to do in the morning.

I slid into another fantasy fugue state. I was in a forest. A birch forest in Russia. In the Sparrow Hills. Out of somewhere—some long-forgotten class at college—that name entered my mind. It was cold, a late-afternoon winter sunset blazing orange against spiky black branches, lighting the edges of high cirrus clouds. I was tied to a tree with the singer from the Fine Young Cannibals. Shadowy forms were menacing us. Men in big fur hats. Something like that.

I didn't like walking home after midnight, but Washington is not New York. Good luck finding a taxi. And I just didn't feel like calling one on the phone. Back at Winslow, we had automatic dial car privileges if we worked after 10:00 P.M. We used to abuse the service and use the cars like limousines to take us around to nightclubs. There was a crackdown at some point, I recall. No more subsidized ferrying to Balthazar.

So there I was, walking down the deserted street behind the Supreme Court Building. Marshall had once offered to give me a pistol to carry. A Colt Mustang .380. But I passed. Once you start toting a gun, you have to have it with you all the time. The one time you leave it at home is the one time you'll need it, and all the hassle and felony risk of carrying it around will have been in vain. And I have enough trouble just getting dressed in the morning.

I made the corner of East Capitol unmolested. I hadn't seen a soul since I left the office. That's Washington. Early to bed, early to rise. Dorks and dweebs—a whole city of them. Squirrels. Mousy schoolmarms. They come from all over the country to be here. Washington, Dork Central. Dweeb magnet. I twirled down my block like I was spinning on ice, my briefcase an outflung counterweight. There was no one to see me. I ran up the steps to my building, the name of one of the Founding Fathers in script over the door. When I reached my apartment, I saw there were five messages waiting on my answering machine. I didn't play them. I called Marshall, woke him up.

"You ignored me today," I said.

"What time is it?"

"It's only one. I want you to come over."

"Now?"

"Absolutely now. Are you defying me?"

"No. I suppose not."

"Absolutely not. Get over here. Bring your razor."

"I'll shave."

"Under my supervision."

"I'm sorry about that."

"Noted."

there's something about a Range Rover, crappy British engineering notwithstanding. We were out in Virginia, Marshall and I, heading along I-66 somewhere near Manassas. Manasshole, I've heard it named. Town house hell. Towne homes, the Realtors call them. Shitboxes in the middle of reclaimed cow pastures, with a view of Wal-Mart. Miles and miles of them. I was a world away from that, sealed in our expensive four-wheeler as if I were traversing the Serengeti. My walking ATM of a boyfriend in the driver's seat. Arditti Quartet on the CD player. Climate control. Portable computer providing real-time currency exchange rates. Cristal in a cooler. A couple of real buttwads, the mall rat in me was saying.

But he had the common touch, too. And I liked that about him. There was beer in with the Cristal. And this Rover was full of guns. Just like the pickups parked in the cow pastures. We were going to do some shooting, a ways down the road. Then a picnic, somewhere in the country.

"I owned an MG once," I said. "A little white one. It was constantly down. Do you have that problem?"

"I've gotten good service from this thing. So far. When did you have a car?"

"In college. And afterward. I sold it when I moved to Manhattan."

"Really."

"My dad gave it to me my second year at Kenyon. I said I needed a car."

"And he gave you an MG."

"Well, it was used."

"And a load of trouble."

"It was. There was a boy at Kenyon who could fix it for me."

"I bet."

"He was rewarded for his time."

"I can imagine."

He didn't need to imagine, since the same rewards were his on a regular basis.

"You still haven't heard from your dad?" he asked.

"No."

"You have no idea where he is?"

"No."

"Is that hard for you?"

"I suppose it is."

He put on his sunglasses. I put mine on, too.

"What did you study at college?" he asked me. "What'd you major in?"

"History."

"History. I didn't know that."

"I bounced around. That's what I ended up with enough credits in."

"History."

"You didn't know. I told Lucius."

"Lucius."

"We talk all the time."

"You mean he talks."

"He loves to hear his own voice."

"What does he tell you?"

"Oh, let's see. What does he talk about? Just a random sampling of subjects? Life in Canada. The Elgin Marbles. White SNCC groupies—"

"One of his favorites."

"I've noted a certain testiness on his part regarding black people. What's that all about?"

"I think it was the riot at Columbia."

"When I was in law school there, I saw a film about that riot."

"Lucius was a sophomore, if I've got it right. But he was totally into it. It was burn, baby, burn."

I laughed. The very idea.

"Then," Marshall said, "the Black Power kids kicked all the white lefties out of Hamilton Hall. I don't think he ever got over it. Then there's all his time in South Africa. Maybe bad attitudes are rubbing off on him."

"Speaking of South Africa."

"Let's not."

"I think I hit it off with Van Zyk."

"We have to be careful with Van Zyk."

"Why?"

"He's a bit volatile."

Something in the back of my head told me to be wily and subtle here, but it wasn't my style.

"Volatile? How?"

"He goes off half-cocked."

"Did he steal the escrow money?"

"No one stole anything. That money was moved to another account."

"That was news to Lucius. The day it happened, anyway."

"It was my fault. I hadn't told him."

We were exiting 66 onto Route 29, the road to Charlottesville. Passing from the environs of D.C. into real rural Virginia. The question I was about to ask, concerning the FBI, drifted away to the margins of my consciousness. I was more interested in the car in front of us, which had a bumper sticker warning that the driver was certified for the Rapture, and liable to be hoovered up to heaven on extremely short notice.

"I should go to church," I said.

"Maybe I'll join you."

I knew he hated his church. He was raised Presbyterian, and once I accompanied him to a service in D.C. He hadn't been to one in many, many years, he had said. There'd been some changes. The first thing he noticed was that "Onward,

Christian Soldiers" was gone from the hymnal. The Sunday morning tedium of his churchgoing youth had been broken only by the occasional opportunity to sing "Onward, Christian Soldiers," and they had taken even that small pleasure away. There were other changes. Gone was the Westminster Catechism, and the stern Calvinist patriarch of his youth had been replaced by an androgynous escapee from the Esalen Institute, a cosmic squishbag who loved all, served all, but reserved a special affection for the residents of Palestine and Nicaragua. During the sermon, the words "empower" and "empowerment" were employed, by my count, nine times. We left as we were being directed to hug one another. Since they hadn't passed the plate yet, my lesson in contemporary mainline Protestantism cost him only forty-five minutes and a queasy stomach.

"So you want to start going to Mass?" I asked.

"With you I might."

"You just want to see me on my knees."

One thing this particular Range Rover was not good for was road sex. In that regard Marshall seemed to have English priorities. It was too hard to lean across the gap between the seats, what with the car phone and this other *device,* some kind of satellite scrambler or something. I didn't want to ask.

"Well, we know that's the one place we could go together in public and know that none of our associates would ever spot us."

"True."

"Actually, there's one other place."

Which we were pulling into at that moment. The Roney Brothers Sports Emporium. A gun store, in other words.

With a shooting range out back. Marshall nosed between two pickup trucks at the edge of the lot.

"Aren't you ashamed of yourself, pulling up here in this vehicle?"

"A bit. But my truck's in Charlottesville."

At least we were dressed for the occasion. I was wearing a vintage flannel shirt I'd gotten a few pounds ago, and I was afraid I was going to burst the buttons. I was ready for the stares. One thing about rednecks: they don't pretend they're not interested in what you have to offer.

"How ya doing, Marshall?"

The proprietor was all smiles. I felt better, now that I knew we were welcome. I thought of Zanesville, and that world my sisters were always dodging when we were teenagers: the world of dirt bikes, convenience stores, and *Minitruckin'* magazine. A world where my tits were worth their weight in gold.

"Billy, this is my lawyer, Rosalind Wilcox."

"Lawyer? You gonna sue me?"

"We want to shoot a few rounds."

"What can I do you?"

"Nine millimeter, .44 special, .357."

"All right."

"Give me fifty rounds of nine, and twenty each of the other two."

I could hear shots from the range out back. So loud. That's the shocking thing, the first time you shoot a little pistol. How loud it is.

"Here, sweetheart." Marshall handed me a set of ear protectors. They looked like old-time stereo headphones.

"She know the drill?" That was Billy, addressing Marshall.

"Rosalind is an expert."

I was Rosie in my youth; in law school I became Rosalind and I permitted no backsliding. Only my mother could call me Rosie. My sisters were required to adhere to the new regime.

"We'll shoot the nine first."

There were five shooting lanes; two were occupied, and Marshall and I would be sharing a third, since we were going to be shooting alternately with the same guns. We started with the Beretta, four clips of ten. The thing would hold fourteen, but Marshall loaded only ten bullets each time. So we shot twenty rounds each. I had fourteen shots inside the body of the man-sized silhouette: five in the head and neck, seven in the chest, and two in the poor thing's privates. All twenty of Marshall's were in the head and chest.

"You wouldn't even think of shooting him where I did," I said. He didn't laugh.

Then it was six shots each with the Charter Arms .44 Special. A lousy gun, in my view. Too much buck, not enough bang. Plus I missed the body four out of six times. I was feeling the urge for a cigarette. While Marshall loaded up the Smith & Wesson .357, I walked away for a smoke.

Two guys were already puffing away, in their camouflage vests and baseball caps. Not worn backward, you can be sure of that. One of them gave me a light, and we made small talk while their eyes darted from my lips to my breasts and back again. After a while they resumed a conversation that I had interrupted by arriving.

"So we been robbed," one of them said.

"Reckon so," said the other.

We been robbed. That phrase chimed in my head. Where had I heard it? Marshall was beckoning me; it was time to shoot our last go-round. Six shots each with the police revolver.

"Make it good," he said.

I sighted down the barrel. I thought of Drew Gillespie. Drew and my father, lined up with their pistols. Dad didn't particularly seem to like Drew, not the way Mom did. But then Dad never seemed to like anyone. His approval was hard to come by. But he and Drew both liked guns, and one day I watched them square off against a bunch of old bowling pins. They had me set the pins up, and they shot them down as fast as their .45s could pop off the rounds. Drew won. Not many people beat my father at anything. Drew did. At that one thing.

The pistol kicked hard. I aimed again. And it came to me. *So we've been robbed.* That was Marshall. Marshall had said that when he came back from L.A. and found out the escrow account was empty.

"Fuck," I said aloud.

"You're doing fine." Marshall shouted so I could hear through the protectors.

I put the last three shots right between the eyes.

"regular or extra large?"

That was Claudia, forcing me to face the big questions. We were ordering in. Another junk food orgy. We were getting ready for the closing on the Xantex deal.

"I'm going vegetarian," I said. Who was I kidding?

"Yeah, and I'm taking the veil."

This job had its occupational hazards. How could I lose weight? Look at my lunches over the last couple of weeks.

Steak and butter-drenched lobster at the Palm; fried calamari and salmon fillet in a honey-mustard glaze at the Monocle; summer truffle butterbombs, goose liver terrine, and veal with duxelles in cream sauce at La Colline; an "Atomica" at Pizza Paradiso, along with more than my share of a bottle of Merlot; not to mention—but I will mention—a mess of fried chicken livers at Georgia Brown's. What's a girl to do? I can't go in those places and order salad. Jesus.

Not that I did any better on my own. Nachos at the Green Beard, cheeseburgers at the Tune Inn, spicy wings from Popeyes. Holy Christ. Personal trainer time.

"I made a distribution of the last changes," Claudia said. "They're supposed to fax comments by seven."

"They" were Xantex's house counsel—lately of Johannesburg, now ensconced in a temporary office in Miami for the weeks leading to the closing—and our outside counsel. (Half-Smoke. Whom I'd just set up with Valerie. We'd see how that went. A closing of a different kind.) Plus a lawyer on Grand Cayman. Xantex's outside counsel in London wouldn't respond until tomorrow morning. Claudia and I had all the closing documents sorted in piles on a worktable. Each document had to go to nine different outside offices for review and comment. Usually I was just one of the busybody commentators. But on this deal we were the lead underwriter. It was our baby. The stress was making me crave salt and grease.

"What's the big idea," I bitched to no one in particular, since our bosses were not on the premises, "scheduling a closing on Halloween, anyway? And on a Sunday!"

"Life in the fast lane."

"This is such bullshit."

Said Sunday was only three days away.

"We aren't going to make it," I said.

"They always reschedule them, anyway."

"That's true. But not until we've stayed up all night for a week to get ready."

"Hey, but if we didn't think we had to get this done by Sunday, would we ever get it done?"

"Of course not."

"There you go."

The fax blizzard finally subsided around ten. I was sitting with a cigarette, watching Claudia sort the paper piles.

"I can't get over you and Marshall," she said.

"Was it really a surprise?"

"It was."

"Good. I've never done this before."

"What?"

"Keep a secret. I feel strange. Subversive."

"What do you know about him?"

"Marshall?"

"Yeah."

"Know like what?"

"Like was he married? Is he married?"

"He was. He has a kid. A grown daughter. She's at Brown. Or she was. She graduated. I guess she's been graduated awhile, actually."

"Have you met her?"

"No."

"How about the wife?"

"They divorced a long time ago. In 1974, I think. A few years after he came home from Laos."

"So where is she?"

"In Maine."

"Maine."

"She lives on Mount Desert Island."

"Woo-woo."

"Oh, yeah, there's money in the picture. But what I don't get is: Marshall wasn't rich when they divorced. He'd just left the government and was doing the M.B.A. thing at Wharton. I guess he has family money."

"I knew he was at Wharton. I didn't know when."

"I think he just missed Michael Milken."

"And he never remarried."

"Not to my knowledge."

"What do you talk about?"

Good question. One thing we hadn't discussed was the FBI.

"Sometimes we talk about Lucius."

"There's a piece of work."

"Has he ever come on to you?"

"Lucius?"

"Yeah."

"Not really. No."

"Not really. You think he's gay?"

"I don't know. You think?"

"I don't know. He doesn't seem to have a girlfriend."

"Well, he asked me once about you."

"About me?"

"Yeah. He asked me if you had a boyfriend."

"And?"

"Well, I didn't know. At the time."

"And now that you do know, you shut up."

"Right. And then he less than subtly suggested you might be—well, sapphic."

"What?"

"He said something."

"That I'm double-gaited?"

"Something like that. The word was 'sapphic.' And here we are wondering if he's gay."

"Gay men just are. A lesbian is something you become. You can tell him I'm working on it."

"Have you ever been with a girl?"

"You mean, done it with a woman?"

"That's what I mean."

"No. I subscribe to the Gnostic notion that men and women complete each other." I decided not to share a late-night encounter I had at Winslow one time. There was this legal assistant in the office, a zaftig little thing we called R2D2. A shorter version of myself, minus the cover-girl face. She'd roll into a room like a fire hydrant on casters, leading with her breasts. And Christ, if she didn't fall for me, too. Actually tried to kiss me one night, after midnight, when we were working on some distribution for a closing, the way Claudia and I were now, marking up documents for hours. Kiss me if you must, I said, and then we need to get back to work. "Not that it isn't fun to tease the dykes now and again. They're so easy to jerk around if you're a woman yourself. How about you?"

"Once. In college. I was so drunk I can hardly remember."

"That describes most college sex."

"I envy you, having a regular boyfriend. I want one. It's been over a year since I broke up with Nigel. It's time."

"What happened with Nigel?"

"We got to that point where you either make some declarations or you break up."

"Got you."

"We broke up."

"Yeah. God. Those declarations. Two of my sisters are

married, and a third is engaged. She goes around referring to her 'fiancé'—my fiancé this, my fiancé that. It's like her brain turned to stewed tomatoes. I can't stand it."

"Well, there doesn't seem to be much chance of acquiring a fiancé in this town."

"Wonks and weenies."

"You said it."

"My sister's fiancé is funny, though. I can tell he has a crush on me."

"Maybe he's marrying your sister just so he can see you at Thanksgiving."

"No, but he is funny. I was teasing him about getting married, and he said, 'Look, I'm not giving up any James Bond bachelor paradise.' He said, 'You know what being single meant for me? It meant sitting alone with a bag of Chee-Tos and my dick in my hand, waiting for the dishes to wash themselves.'"

Claudia laughed.

"Why don't we pack it in for tonight?"

"Just let me xerox these cover pages."

I picked up the construction contract for the power plant, just to feel the heft. It was three hundred pages, without its accompanying volumes of supporting materials, and it was full of endless unreadable clauses and codicils that could cost the unwary millions of dollars. It had been drafted by Xantex's counsel in London. They could have pulled it all out of their collective ass, still steaming. How would I possibly know? How would anyone?

"Did you ask Marshall about the FBI?"

"I can't seem to get around to it."

"Come on. You're lovers."

"Makes it worse."

I flipped through our credit agreement with Xantex, terrorist provisions and all. I looked at the escrow clauses. That empty Swiss account should contain more than 10 million bucks by now. Maybe I should get on a plane to Chiasso.

Claudia handed me a new cover page. "You think there's something funny going on?"

"Do you?"

"Well, I don't know. That whole business, 'offshore money.' Has a creepy feel."

"It just means we serve foreign investors. We provide a conduit between foreign capital markets and U.S. underwriters."

"What does that really mean?"

Claudia was sharp. And only twenty-four. What did it mean? We had hundreds of millions of dollars sluicing through our operation. All of it from overseas investors. I once asked Lucius how he became an independent investment banker, and he said a lucky conversation with a guy at the next urinal. That guy was Marshall. It occurred to me now that he was begging the question.

"Well," I said, "here's how it works. This Xantex deal, now. There's a diamond mine."

"Yeah."

"And there's a power plant that supplies electricity for the mine."

"Yeah."

"We're putting money into the power plant, in return for a share of the future revenues from the sale of the electricity. The biggest customer for the electricity from this particular plant is the Garworks diamond mine, largely owned by De Beers."

"Yeah."

"Except that we have money in the mine, too. So we're making out, coming and going. We're paying ourselves for electricity."

"So what's the catch?"

"No catch."

"Why the fuss over the contract?"

"Oh, there's this argument over force majeure."

"Which means?"

"Which means events beyond the control of the parties to the contract. Acts of God. I've been pushing them to put in a clause covering terrorist activity, and for some reason they've been balking."

"Why would they balk at that?"

"I don't know."

And I didn't, I realized.

"You all set?" I asked.

"Just have to get my bike."

Claudia had a nifty little folding bike with half-size wheels that she used to ride back and forth to her apartment on Lincoln Park. She could stow it in the ground-floor coat closet.

"Are you sure you don't want a taxi? It's late." I was a little concerned about her, even on a bike. Bad things sometimes happened on Capitol Hill.

"I'll be all right."

We locked the doors and punched on the alarm system. No lobby, no desk guard. We were it.

"How come Winslow isn't doing these distributions?"

Claudia was wondering why the two of us were so mired in scut work when we could be paying several thousand dollars an hour to have someone else do it.

"They will be, on the final round. But for some reason

Lucius wanted us to assemble everything first, so he can look at it tomorrow."

"He's never made us do this before."

"I know."

"There's something weird about this deal."

"I don't know."

"Isn't there?"

"I don't know. Maybe."

"Why does the FBI get interested in banks?"

"We're not exactly a bank."

"But we can launder money."

Honestly that had never occurred to me. We were partnered in project finance deals with big reputable underwriters. We raised money from foreign insurance companies, foreign pension funds.

Some of the money, anyway.

"It's probably a tax thing, if it's anything at all."

"I don't think the FBI worries about tax evaders. Wouldn't the IRS be calling us first?"

"Don't ask, don't tell," I said.

"Do you know anything about anything like that?"

"No, I don't. It never even occurred to me. I've never thought about it."

"Well, me neither, until lately. But you know, strange people are calling, asking for Lucius. And Marshall. People who don't sound like Wharton graduates."

"You're such an elitist."

"Not elite enough."

We were at the corner of Second and A.

"I'll walk with you for another block."

A block and a half down A we came up to the alley at Miller's Court, which led to the back of my building.

"See you tomorrow."

"Okay. Be safe."

She pedaled off, east down A Street. In the daylight it was a wonderful walk. There were a lot of trees along the brick sidewalks, and all sorts of fantastically varied nineteenth-century row house facades. Walking that street on a sunny day made me glad I lived in Washington. At night it was a different story.

I stepped into the cobblestone alleyway, under sodium vapor light. A tangle of overhead electrical wires threw sharp shadows on the ancient carriage house garage doors. Ahead, in the far distance, I could see car headlights on Pennsylvania Avenue. There was a prickling sensation on the back of my neck. I whirled around, suddenly convinced that I was being followed. The alley stretched away, empty. I backed up a few paces, looking left and right into the interstices between the carriage houses. Nothing. I trotted to East Capitol and the front door of my building. Now my heart was hammering. But I stood on the stoop, convinced that someone was going to round the corner from the alley. Someone who'd been watching me. I had to know.

No one came. Silly paranoia, fueled by Claudia's fantasies. I walked up the five flights of stairs to my apartment. Good exercise. There were no messages on my answering machine. That was unusual.

I kicked off my shoes and picked up the old Lyon & Healy mandolin I'd gotten in college. A holdover from my violin lessons as a child. One day when I was nine Dad came home with five student-model fiddles. It seemed we girls were going to learn to play. There were a couple of years of lessons—a Marx Brothers farce. Something stuck, though, because at Kenyon I fell in with some bluegrassers and took up the mandolin. It was relaxing. I tried some Irish tunes, what I could remember. "Drowsy Maggie" and "Temperance Reel" and "The Battle of Aughrim." My calluses weren't what they used to be. After just a few songs, my fingers were killing me.

I thought about Kenyon, about walking up Middle Path with my father when he bought me the MG. And another time, visiting my sister at Penn—standing on Locust Walk with him, listening to his announcement that he was moving out of the house. That things at home had become unmanageable. I thought he was just talking about Mom. About marriage. I figured midlife crisis, fling with his receptionist, the usual. But it was not the usual. Not by a long shot. What is it about the men in my life that the FBI always wants to speak to them?

The phone rang.

It was a quarter to twelve, and I hesitated a moment before picking up the receiver. But it could be Marshall, I decided.

"Hey, babe," I said, taking a shot in the dark.

There was silence for a moment. My blood pressure surged.

"Hello?" I said.

"Hello?" There was another pause. "Rosie?"

"This is Rosalind. Who is this?"

"Drew."

"Drew?"

"Drew Gillespie. Come on. It's me."

"Drew!"

My heart rate escalated. Quite a bit, actually.

"How are you?" he asked.

"I'm good. I guess. Where are you?"

"I'm here."

"Here?"

"In Washington."

"What are you doing in Washington?"

"I don't know. Had a little time on my hands. Your message got me thinking."

I was thinking, too. About Marshall. About how inconvenient this all might rapidly become.

"Oh, right. I've been thinking about my dad. I wanted to ask you something."

"What?"

"Something about his Swiss bank account."

"Oh yeah, that."

"How did you find out about that?"

"Can we meet somewhere?"

"Yeah, I guess."

There was silence on the line.

"How's Zanesville?" I asked.

"Oh, you know."

"Yeah. I know. That's why I left."

Silence again.

"So you want to meet," I said.

"Sure. We have a lot of catching up to do."

"What are you doing?"

"Same thing. Westrall wants me to buy his body shop, but I don't know."

"So you're still doing the thing with the cars?" I could see the shiny paint, feel the soft redone seats of a classic machine.

"Oh, yeah."

"Whatcha got?"

"I just turned around a '65 Mustang. And a '49 Merc."

"Oh, cool. You have one for me?"
"A '56 T-Bird. Your favorite, if I remember."
"I could never decide between that one and the '57."
"Got one of those, too."
"Oh, that I want to see."
"Anytime."
"I'm still a lawyer, I'm afraid."
"Making that good money, I guess. I was keeping up with you, until your mother left town."

Mother and Drew. There was something between them. Even though he wasn't M.B.A. material. Not like my sisters' husbands. None of them were hometown boys.

"I'm sorry I didn't write, Drew. But I don't know. It seemed best."
"You ever think of me?"
"Sometimes."
"You aren't married, I guess."
"I'm not, no. You?"
"No."
"Have a girlfriend?"
"Not at the moment."
"Is that why you're calling me?"
"I'm calling because you called me. And you sounded a little concerned about something."
"Well, I guess I am."
"You wanted to talk about your father."
"Yes. Yes, I did."
"And I know you. Something's wrong."
"Nothing's wrong."
"But nothing's right."
"I didn't say that."

"I got a phone message after three years of radio silence. You want to explain it?"

Time to tap-dance.

"Not exactly."

"What does that mean?"

"Let's just figure out a time to meet."

"I'm free all day. And night."

"I'm very busy at work right now. I've got a big closing coming up."

"Closing."

"A deal involving a power plant and a diamond mine in Africa."

"Some real money there, I guess."

"Real money. Yes."

"I'd like to hear about it."

"It's boring."

"Doesn't sound boring to me. Not like a dented fender."

"I don't know, Drew."

"Well, if you're too busy, Rosie."

"Rosalind. I go by Rosalind now."

"That's right. I like that better."

"Maybe we can have a quick drink."

"That would be good. You know, after I got your message I went out to look at Big Muskie. You know, they've closed that mine down."

"I didn't know that."

"Yeah, shut her down."

"Not Big Muskie!"

"Shut her down."

"Times change."

"And they've filled up the Rosedale mine. Got a park there

now. I went over there, too. Lay down, right where we used to."

"Drew."

"Just lay down in the dark and looked at the stars through the tree branches."

I was quiet.

"A bunch of squirrels were jumping around up in the high limbs, making them rock and swish. I was thinking about you."

I made a date with him. The next afternoon, Friday, at the Tabard Inn. I told him where it was, what kind of place it was.

"I don't think I've seen anything prettier than those squirrels," he said, "jumping across each other in the starlight and shaking the leaves down out of the sky."

"god *damn* it!"

I was rolling around on the floor, trying to untwist my panty hose. What a fucking mess my apartment was. Thirty-two years old—less than a month away from thirty-three—and I couldn't find my shoes, I didn't have an unwrinkled blouse, there were dirty dishes in the sink. I was almost as old as Christ when he died. House counsel, making a hundred and fifty grand. The maid's regular visit was later today.

But dirt wasn't the problem—the problem was my stuff strewn all over. She couldn't even clean up because I'd left junk all over the dresser tops, all over the chairs, all over the floor, all over the bed.

"*Fuck!*"

Drew's news about Big Muskie made me sad. That surprised me, my being sad about such a thing. This blast from Zanesville, a place I was trying to put behind me. It was my own fault: I called him. Now I was going to have to fit him into my crazy week.

I wanted a cigarette.

Big Muskie was a huge digging machine, the largest dragline shovel in the world. It was red and cream and as big as a two-story house. Drew and I used to sneak into the mine pit late at night and creep right up next to the giant. He'd hold me from behind while I looked up at the stars along the knife edge of the cab roof. "AEP," said the big logo way up over our heads. That stood for American Electric Power.

"Shit."

No cigarettes. Luckily there was a pharmacy right at the end of my block. And a corner liquor store right across the street from that. I finally dressed myself, procured a pack of Marlboros, and, thus fortified, made it to my desk just before 10:00 A.M. I was thinking about a funny thing: American Electric Power was a sometime client of ours. Rigel Associates had occasionally funneled money to the owners of Big Muskie. Life was so strange sometimes.

There was already a message backlog. Xantex's London counsel had been working overtime.

"You know, there's no way we can wrap this up by Sunday," I said. I was addressing my speakerphone, and my voice was emerging both upstairs and at Marshall's hideaway on Calvert Street.

"Yes, I know," Lucius said.

"Did you know that yesterday?"

"Had an inkling."

"Well, what are we going to do?"

"We'll put off the closing. We're going to want to do it in New York, anyway. See if you can schedule a conference room at Winslow, sometime next week."

"My pleasure."

Chewing my thumbnail.

"What we have so far looks good," Lucius said. "I'm comfortable turning this over to Winslow for the ride out. Marshall?"

"Fine with me. Thank you, Rosalind."

"You're welcome."

"Rosalind, can you come up to my office?" That was Lucius.

"Be right up."

I stopped in to see Claudia.

"We're off the hook," I said.

"They postponed the closing."

"They're going to."

"Hooray."

"I'm going in to talk to Lucius right now."

"What's your boyfriend say?"

"Shhhhhhh! Verboten!"

"Sorry."

"I mean it."

"Okay. I know. Omerta."

"Amen."

I went in to face Lucius. His hair seemed grayer. He'd put on ten years when I wasn't looking.

"Can I ask you something?" he said.

"Why do people employ that particular interrogatory? It's not as if there's any chance I'm going to say no."

"It's a convention. Used to slide over awkwardness. And with you, there's always a chance you'll say no."

"Actually, I say yes way too easily."

"So I noticed."

"Let's just forget about that, okay?"

"Okay."

"What do you want to ask me?"

"Have you ever spoken to the FBI?"

"What? What do you mean?"

"Have you ever had an interview with an FBI agent?"

"I talked to an FBI recruiter once. I don't know if she was an actual agent or not."

"How about in connection with your father? Did the feds ever contact you?"

"No. I was in law school when all that went down. They didn't get around to me. The Ohio State Police talked to my older sister. And my two youngest sisters. The FBI may have talked to my mother. I know they called her when my father disappeared."

"But nothing since?"

"Nothing. Why? What's going on?"

He made a steeple of his fingers, resting his chin on the tips.

"Has your father ever tried to get in touch with you?"

"You mean, since I came to Washington?"

"Yes."

"I told you. No. He disappeared in 1994. No one in my family has heard from him."

"He skipped bail."

"Well, yes. What has this got to do with anything?"

Now he leaned back, with his hands behind his head.

"You know, a few years ago I asked to see my FBI file. I made an FOIA request."

"You have an FBI file?"

"I did. You know, after I was arrested at Columbia."

"Oh, right."

"They had everything in there. My subscription to *Granma*. My SDS membership. My residence change to Canada."

"It's nice that somebody cared." I didn't add *draft dodger*. He was riding me again. There was this unspoken thing between us. And it wasn't friendly.

"Isn't it, though? Even though I was no threat to anyone, way out there all alone on the banks of the Yukon. Just the flat gray river and the landscape like Siberia. That's what I liked about it, because back in the capital the purges were under way. I used to curl up at night and savor it, being in a backwater while Rome burned. It made me feel close to my old man, even though he wouldn't talk to me. I was wondering how close you feel to your dad."

"Your dad was ashamed of you?"

"The air force was his life. I was a great disappointment."

"He'd be proud of you now."

"Think your dad could be in Canada?"

"He could be anywhere."

"It was really something. That part of Canada. We're talking about the southern Arctic. There were these old steamboats pulled up on the riverbank there. Stern-wheelers.

Ancient. You wouldn't believe it. Totem poles. I could look out my window at the headwaters of the Yukon and I could see the old world. I could see my father, right after the war. The real war. The war we won. My father was a lucky man. Out there in Alaska, pioneer for the empire. Jet planes and the new age. Sonic booms. The late forties was the time to be alive."

"So you were born just in time."

"Not quite soon enough. I was too young to really remember those years in Alaska."

I knew he'd been born on an air base in Alaska. And I knew what was coming.

"Land of my birth," he said. "Western Canada was like crawling back into the womb."

Canada. This wasn't the first time I'd heard this Whitehorse story. And it wasn't the first time he'd asked me if I thought my father was up north of the border. I remembered the first time. I'd only been on the job two months, and the business about being alone in Whitehorse was grafted onto an unsolicited lecture about the effect of women on male-dominated environments like investment banking. He was explaining me to myself, as he loved to do, and at the end of it I had to go to the library and look up the Venus of Willendorf. Boy was I pissed when I saw her.

"I've heard this before, Lucius."

"So you have. Listen, if the FBI happens to call, don't talk to them without letting me know, okay?"

"Okay."

He looked at me.

"What's on your mind, Lucius?"

"Have you ever read *Absalom, Absalom!*? The Faulkner novel?"

"In college."

"Did Thomas Sutpen remind you of anyone?"

I just looked back at him, my blood pressure rising. Why had I always felt I'd known Lucius longer than I had? Known him and loathed him?

"I'm going downstairs now," I said.

"Be productive."

Back in my office I got Marshall on the phone.

"I have to see you," I said, leaving the tease out of my voice.

"Now?"

"Now."

"Let's have lunch."

"That was easy."

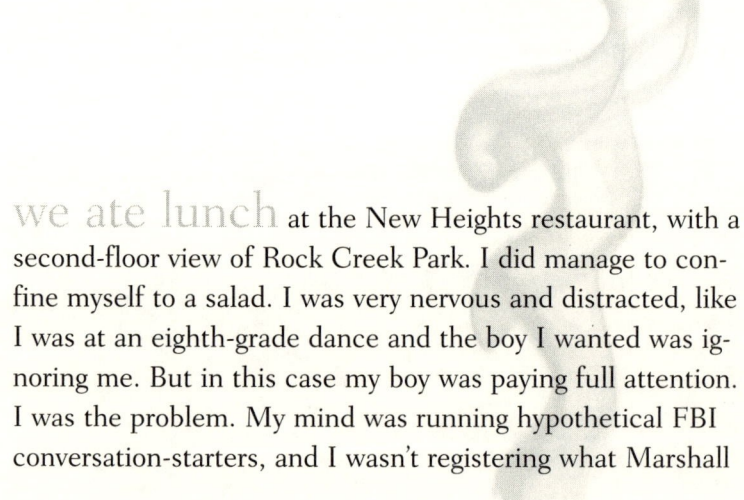

we ate lunch at the New Heights restaurant, with a second-floor view of Rock Creek Park. I did manage to confine myself to a salad. I was very nervous and distracted, like I was at an eighth-grade dance and the boy I wanted was ignoring me. But in this case my boy was paying full attention. I was the problem. My mind was running hypothetical FBI conversation-starters, and I wasn't registering what Marshall was saying. There was just a droning buzz, something about LIBOR-linked bonds and contingency financing facilities.

"Are you listening to me, darling?"

"No, I'm not. Sorry."

"What's the matter?"

I folded my hands and frowned like a remonstrative nun.

"Why is the FBI interested in Rigel Associates?"

At first I thought Marshall was going to blow it off with a joke, but then he took my hand and said, "Let's go to my office."

He looked like a man face-to-face with God.

"Excuse me for a second," I said.

He paid up while I ran to the ladies' room for a lipstick update. I stared in the mirror, at my father's blue eyes, at my mother's thick black hair, thinking: we could have beautiful children.

Outside on Calvert, he took my hand again. This was unprecedented. I almost jerked away.

"Uh, we're in public," I said.

"I know. I don't care."

I was *claimed*. And I felt it: the curse of regularity. The effect was instantaneous; the erotic energy began draining from our relationship. Right away. With every step we took. I could feel it radiating into space, shooting out the top of my head. What was wrong with me?

Marshall read my thoughts.

"You don't like this, do you?"

"I don't know."

"You liked things clandestine."

"Oh, they're still clandestine."

He dropped my hand. I felt flustered, and the erotic

energy level started recovering. Halfway up the office steps, I stuck my tongue in his ear.

"You started it," I said.

When we finished, I had a bruise on my back from the edge of his desk.

"You were going to tell me about the FBI," I said, sliding back into my brassiere.

"Let's take a walk," he said.

"You're in a romantic mood."

"I need a shower."

"So do I."

"We're on the same page today."

halfway through one of those microdistillery whiskeys from the Kentucky backwoods, after a shower and some spiced shrimp from his Sub-Zero, Marshall started telling me a story. I was looking out the living room window of his house on Cathedral Avenue, watching the leaves swirl down from the oaks and maples. Two days until Halloween. I was thinking I should do something for my niece and nephew.

"When I was in Vientiane, I met a man named Arlie Ralston. A Brit. He was one of those people you always find on the fringes of a postcolonial war, somebody who'd figured out a way to make money out of misery. He was connected in Hong Kong banking circles. His dealings with me were brief. He wanted an introduction to some Hmong tribesmen. He wanted to offer them some contract work. Courier work, it turned out. He wanted people to carry pouches of cash out of Thailand. That's all. Once it got to Vientiane, he took care of getting it to Hong Kong. I guess he peeled off some percentage for his trouble."

I thought of mosquito netting. Jungle sunsets. The Plain of Jars.

"This was drug money? Heroin money?"

"I presume. Opium. That was the business. The point is, years later, when I got out of Wharton, I got a call from another Brit, named Trevor Langford. He'd been talking to Arlie, they were old buddies, and my name had come up."

My mind was on that mosquito netting. Army cots. Military webbing.

"Well, Trevor had a proposition for me. Legitimate. Wholly above-board. Nothing to do with narco profits. It seems he had a line on a big capital geyser out of Johannesburg. Diamond money, looking for foreign shelters. Untainted, he claimed, and as far as I ever found out, he was right. But he, and his people in Johannesburg, didn't like the fee structure of the deals they'd been offered by established investment firms. I was at First Boston at the time. I was happy to leave."

"That's how you got started."

"That's how I got started. One thing led to another, and I hooked up with Lucius."

"At a urinal, I recall."

"Yes. Well, back to Trevor. He funneled us our first deals, pretty small stuff—thirty, fifty, sixty million dollars. But it got us into the game. And then we started getting Hong Kong deals, from Arlie."

"Where's Arlie now?"

"London. Semiretired. House in Holland Park and another in Cornwall."

"Does he need a wife?"

"He's had three."

"Oh."

I recalled another Brit, a boy I was two-timing Jay Hixon with back at Winslow. The one who liked to choke me during sex. I wondered what he was up to these days.

"So, anyway, Trevor drops off the map, we're not doing much business with him anymore, and I really pretty much forget about him. Then, last spring, I get a call from the FBI."

I opened the drawer of the black walnut desk I was standing before, not looking for anything in particular, just wanting to do something with my hands, and there I saw a pistol, a Sig Sauer .380, a fine piece of Swiss-German design, shiny stainless steel like Marshall's refrigerator.

"There were allegations about an attempt to assume straw control of a British bank," he said. "Trevor, as I understand it, was accused of attempting to recruit Brit front men for the deal."

"Accused?"

"An indictment may be pending. That's all I know."

"Who was allegedly trying to do this? Take over the bank."

"Well, I'm not sure. I heard they were Bulgarian, and I heard they were Indonesian."

I picked up the Sig and pressed the button to release the magazine. It was loaded. I pulled the slide back to clear the chamber.

"Where did you hear all this?"

"At a dinner party."

I aimed out the window. I was thinking: you've never taken me to a dinner party.

"It seems a British court subpoenaed all of Trevor's financial records. And my name was in there. Along with Rigel Associates. Interpol talked to the FBI. So they asked me what I knew about Trevor and this attempted acquisition. The answer was nothing."

There was a metallic dry-fire click as I pulled the trigger.

"End of story?" I asked.

"I hope."

I put the gun back in the drawer and sat down next to Marshall on his Victorian settee. His furniture was an eclectic mix of styles and periods. But it was all high-five-figure stuff. That's what tied it together.

"Arlie and I used to talk a lot in Vientiane. You should have seen it. The most vaporous theorizing went on, in the middle of that deranged war. People dropped names I hadn't heard since my senior philosophy seminar, right in the middle of the contract killings and the drug deals and the slave trafficking."

"Slave trafficking?"

"Prostitutes."

"I see."

"Arlie predicted the future. And he was right."

"What did he predict?"

"One of his favorite jags was that Germany would reunite in our lifetime. This was '69, '70, he was saying this. Twenty years later it happened. Communism would collapse, he'd say. Even in Asia. Especially in Asia. It was a Western idea, he said. A Jewish idea. When you grafted it onto Asian sensibilities, you got the grotesque teratoma of Maoism. It would die, he said."

Lecture time again. I thought about one of my boyfriends from law school. The one with the doctor bag. The one who passed a pair of handcuffs to me under the restaurant table on our second date. I never put them on. He ended up wearing them. We didn't last long. But he used to deliver endless monologues to me on any subject that came into his head. My problem with men is that something makes me seem to be exactly what they want, and I can't help playing along for a little while. They always think they're just the first man who's really impressed me. And they get so disappointed when they find out the truth.

"Arlie understood, almost before anyone else, that the postwar nuclear standoff between the superpowers, enormously convenient as it was, had become a Maginot Line, antiquated and irrelevant. Events were flowing around it. New markets were springing up, new alliances. He said there was money to be made. He said that a thousand times."

"And he was right."

"Yes, he was."

I looked at my watch. It was three-thirty. I wanted to go to a bar before the happy hour rush kicked in. There's no pleasure like drinking in a dark bar on a workday afternoon while the rest of the world fights with rusting recalcitrant plumbing or pours concrete or slices prosciutto or rides delivery bicycles in the rain or negotiates structured finance deals as interest rates are rising.

I remembered that I had a date. With Drew. Around six or so. I figured I could get a head start.

"Let's go to the Tabard," I said.

We did. During the taxi ride over Marshall told me to forget about the Xantex deal until Monday. Just forget about it. It could wait. London would handle it. The business with the Swiss account was settled.

"Settled? What do you mean, settled?"

"I mean we found the money."

"Where was it?"

He'd show me Monday, he said. In the meantime, we would just share a leisurely weekend together. How about it?

"You'll get no argument from me."

This job was so great.

We sat at the bar in the Tabard Inn on N Street, drinking martinis. The Friday after-work crush gradually built up around us. Things got noisy enough for us to feel very private. I mentioned that an old friend from Zanesville was going to meet us here. A boy I went to high school with.

"Old boyfriend?" asked Marshall.

"I hate that word."

"I've noticed."

"But yes. Old boyfriend. Ancient, actually. It's been ten years."

"Ten years since you've seen him?"

"Oh, I've seen him."

Marshall gave me a look. I kicked him.

"Shut up," I said, though he hadn't said anything. "It's not what you think."

"He married?"

"No."

"Pining for you?"

"Maybe." I kicked him again. "Hey, don't patronize my friends." The whole Zanesville thing stirred something up in me. I drank my second martini too fast. As I got drunk I started to talk about my father. I don't know why. Marshall knew the story in outline. I started filling in some details.

"It was mortifying for my mother."

"I can imagine."

"Just mortifying. More and more stories kept surfacing. It was in the local paper every day. On the local newscasts every night. Luckily Zanesville is a small broadcast market. But eventually it made the *Wall Street Journal*."

"I remember."

"One of their front-page human interest profiles. One of those 'Isn't rural America a trip?' stories. Half of the people accusing my father of things weren't even involved with him. They just wanted to be. Too bad the other half were telling the truth."

"Everyone has a secret life."

I pondered that a moment. I filed it and told myself to follow up later. Then I got back to the story.

"I had no idea. I guess I never thought about it. He was just my dad. We were five girls and my mother, and Dad was this remote figure, out chopping wood or making rounds at the hospital or going hunting or playing poker somewhere. My sisters and I, we were in our own world. We were the Wilcox girls. Known all over Zanesville. Dad would swoop in and out of our lives. He would come in, give us his attention like a precious gift, then turn it off again. He could be a charming man. A real charmer. That didn't come out in the news stories. He would come in sometimes, turn on the charm, and get the whole family wet. Then he'd get pissed, disappointed in something. We didn't measure up. He and

Mom, I know now, were in one of those death struggles that keep some marriages alive. But I was the only one who really loved him, I think. I was the one who wanted to go hunting with him. I think I could have been the son he never had. I wish I'd pushed that harder."

"The Wilcox girls."

"Yeah."

"How old were you when you figured out you were a hot number?"

In truth it was probably a rainy afternoon when I was thirteen. I was looking at a picture history of World War II, at a photograph of two teenage Russian partisans, a boy and a girl, being hanged by Nazi invaders. I kept brushing the tips of my new breasts against the carpet, marveling at the way they filled the space between my chest and the floor, amazed at their mass, at their resilience and extension.

"I don't know if I like the tenor of that question."

"Come on. It's me."

"Oh—eighth grade, I guess. One day I found myself walking down the hall with ten boys. Ten."

I could see the Russian girl choking to death—her head tilted, her mouth slack, her eyes glazed.

"And it hasn't let up since," Marshall said.

It was time to shut this off. I stuck the pointed toe of my shoe into the bottom of his trouser leg. I rocked my foot a couple of times, slowly.

"Oh, I think it has," I said.

"So about your father."

"His real name wasn't Wilcox."

"That I didn't know."

"He was born in Pittsburgh."

"In 1931."

"You did read the news."

"Only after we decided to hire you. I had a researcher run down the stories for me."

"His parents came here in the twenties. From somewhere in the Carpathian Mountains. His father died when he was eight, and he did all sorts of stuff to help support his mother. Dug coal. Worked in the steel mills. At some point he came to Ohio and reinvented himself. New name. M.D. degree. He used the charm and brains he was born with. My mother's family couldn't stand him. Well, at first they liked him, but the romance wore off. They knew where he was from. And when things went sour, they showed no mercy. They called him a hunky, called him white trash, called him all sorts of things. I didn't know any of this. Not any of it. He was my doctor father, distinguished pillar of the community. We were part of the town elite, such as it was."

"Must have been a shock."

"It wasn't. That's the strange part. Not to me it wasn't. I mean, I never suspected anything, but when all the revelations came out, I wasn't shocked. It was like at some secret level I always understood him, and that I was the only one who did. In a perverse way, I was proud of my old man. At least he wasn't square. You know?"

"Yes. I think I do."

"He was molding his world to his own designs, instead of molding himself to fit in. He looked at the people in charge and decided they weren't any better than he was. I think he believed that there's a crime behind every fortune. Do you believe that?"

"I think that's a barroom generalization. The kind of wisdom that comes after four martinis."

"Hey, fuck—" I actually stopped myself. Even though I

was on martini number three. This was Marshall. He had some kind of funny power over me. "Well, he'd seen a lot of scoundrels get rich. I mean, that's how the world works."

"And he decided to get some for himself."

I nodded, watching Marshall stare off into space. My Bombay Sapphire–soaked brain dimly registered that he was undergoing some internal struggle. Some identification, maybe, with the story I was telling?

"There was business with a local bank, I recall," Marshall said. "And something about the county commissioner?"

"Went to jail. Still there, I think. Ratted out my dad in a plea bargain, but then they nailed him on some unrelated charges. I guess they were unrelated. After a while it was hard to tell. It seemed like my dad had his fingers in every scam in the county."

"I remember the sums involved were quite large."

"Huge, actually. Considering."

"Considering what?"

"Considering we're talking about central Ohio."

"Your dad would have felt right at home in our business."

"It's funny, your talking about that Brit pal of yours trying to take over a bank."

"Trevor Langford."

"That's what my dad did. He took over a bank. And a real estate company. And a liquor distributor. Other stuff, too."

"Other stuff."

"Drugs. Slot machines."

"This is getting good."

"He was looking at real jail time."

"That would make a man evaluate his life, I'd say."

"We're talking about the state pen."

"In with the buttfuckers."

"My dad said no way. I'll take my chances as a fugitive. And he got away with it. They've never found him."

"Maybe he'll contact you someday."

"Maybe."

I saw Drew come in. He stood at the step leading down to the bar, looking around. My heart contracted. Shit, there he was. And he looked better than he ever had. Maybe his belt buckle was too big, and maybe he'd never heard of Ermenegildo Zegna. But sharp images came back to me. Starlight on hard rocks. The feel of my palms on his back. I was flooded with love and shame. Of course I was drunk.

"Marshall, this is Drew Gillespie."

They shook hands. Drew was cooler than I thought he'd be. But then he didn't know the deal yet.

"Marshall's my boss."

"You a lawyer, too?" Drew asked.

"No. I'm a banker."

"Banker. Sounds like good money."

"It's money. I won't characterize it further."

I kicked Marshall again. Smart-ass. But I had that happy dizzy feeling.

"Rosie used to be less interested in money," Drew said.

"That's Rosalind," I said.

"Rosalind. Sorry."

"And I'm not that interested in money."

"She's really not," Marshall said.

"See," I said.

"What do you do, Drew?"

"I've done different things. Mostly I restore cars. Classics."

"Just cars?"

"No. A lot of pickup trucks, too. Big market there. And not just with the shitkickers. I sold a few in L.A."

This was news to me. "What, like to celebrities?" I asked.

"Not face-to-face. Those people have people who buy things for them."

"Like pickup trucks."

"If it's the right truck."

"I've got a '63 Chevy Apache." That was Marshall, in full prole mode. Sometimes I liked it, sometimes I didn't. He was referring to the truck in Charlottesville, presumably. I decided not to bring up the Range Rover.

"Oh, cool," said Drew. "I had a '67 GMC, years ago."

"I remember that truck," I said.

"I've got a Ford now. Same year."

"I had a '57 GMC," said Marshall. "How do you like that?"

"That's something."

Jesus Christ.

"It burned up. Had it parked in a barn. Whole mess went up one night."

"Bummer."

"How long are you with us?"

"What do you mean?"

"How long are you staying in D.C.?"

"I don't know. Not long, it looks like."

I ordered another martini.

"Have a drink, Drew," I said.

"I might."

"What'll it be?" Marshall asked.

"Just a beer."

"Drew was a mighty drinker of beer," I said.

"Not anymore," Drew said.

"What happened?"

"I just cut down, that's all."

"You're looking good."

Oh, was he. He was about a year older than I was, which meant he was already thirty-three, thirty-four. I felt the hard arm under his jacket sleeve.

"And we still aren't married," I said. I was speaking generally. I didn't mean "to each other." Did I?

"No."

"No Stephanie in white."

"Nope."

I turned to Marshall. "Drew was engaged once. Her name was Stephanie Granger. It didn't work out."

"I'm sorry," Marshall said.

"No, I'm glad," said Drew.

"What's she doing now?"

"Married and divorced. Moved to Columbus. Works in a nursing home."

Story of a generation. If you miss the train, it's a hard walk down the track.

"I've been telling Marshall about my dad," I said.

"He's famous back home," Drew said.

"So I understand," said Marshall.

"I shouldn't say this," said Drew.

"If you get as far as saying you shouldn't say something, you know you're going to say it. So go ahead."

"There's a pool in Zanesville."

"Some people do know how to swim."

"No, I mean a betting pool. On your dad."

"You mean, like . . . like on what?"

"Where he is."

"What's the favorite line?"

"Mexico."

"Too easy."

"Where do you think he is?" asked Marshall.

"I don't know," said Drew.

"I was just telling Rosalind that I think her father will get in touch with her. Someday."

"Maybe like you, Drew," I said. "Just out of the blue."

Drew looked at us. "He walked on strange streets."

I felt weightless.

"That's what my father said about Dr. Wilcox." Drew was enlightening us. "He walked on strange streets."

Marshall's hand was suddenly in my hair.

"Like father, like daughter," he said.

Then we were kissing. Oh, my God. Right at the bar at the Tabard. And right in front of Drew. I knew I was being a shit, four martinis notwithstanding. So I kissed Drew, too. He got a look on his face. And Marshall. He had a look, too. I'd have to make things up with him. But first I was having a giddy good time, sitting on my barstool with each arm around a different man. I looked at the ceiling and watched it start to spin, slowly. I hoped it wouldn't speed up too much. Now was not the time to be sick.

"Let's drink to the future," I said.

Neither of my men responded.

"Come on!"

Drew left then. I may have started laughing. I hope not. I saw Drew look back at me from the door. I went back to kissing Marshall. We kept at it, right out on N Street. And in the taxi back to Woodley Park. And then I was standing in my underwear again. I was so easily separated from my clothes. I knew I needed to work on that. In Catholic school we were taught to run around outside and engage in vigorous physical activity whenever we were plagued by impure thoughts. To admire God's green works while keeping our clothes on and the temple of our bodies undefiled. I was a bad Catholic. By any reasonable standard. My vigorous physical activity was always the wrong kind.

"I'm too old for this," Marshall said.

"You were great," I lied. "Fantastic."

"Liar."

Well, I *had* found myself thinking of Drew. Down on the banks of the Muskingum River. How we'd done it and how he'd turned me over and done it again, no break; the boy could be a machine sometimes. And there were other things: flashes of Nino in Venice, that Adriatic amusement park. And this: camping on the beach at Castellammare, Nino reclining in the sand while I paid scrupulously rigorous attention to the flexed ligaments of his instep, the articulated point of his finely modeled talus, the hollow at the base of his Achilles tendon swelling into the rounded gastrocnemius, so conducive to osculation, the muscles toned and hardened from either religious workouts or just fortuitous Mediterranean genetics . . .

But mostly I was thinking of Drew. I wanted to get up and go find him. That ridiculous scene at the Tabard. I couldn't leave things that way.

Then I was mad at him again. Who did he think he was, walking into my life? I can't have a life?

"Have you ever been in love?" That was Marshall. Most unexpected.

"I'm in love now," I said. Equally unexpected. I'd never

said that to him before. Of course it had popped out of my mouth a few times over the years, with other men. But what did I mean by it?

"Really? I won't ask with whom."

"I don't know."

"Then I won't push it."

"Let's go to sleep."

"It's eight o'clock."

"I could use a nap before dinner."

"This discussion is just getting interesting."

"All the more reason for a nap."

"Hasn't anyone ever tried to bully you by telling you they loved you?"

"Many times. I've just had to be honest."

"And cruel."

"Well, the truth is the truth."

"My ex-wife once told me the cruelest thing a person can say to another person is 'I'm fond of you, but not that way.'"

"You've never heard that from me."

"I can just imagine you saying it."

I remembered Drew, years ago, standing on the banks of the Muskingum River.

"Why are you getting so gooey on me all of a sudden?" I asked.

"I thought you were the one getting gooey."

"You need me to be cruel?"

"I'm just wondering if I can stand the truth."

"About what?"

"About us."

I was silent. And grouchy. I heard Lucius, his insinuating voice, teasing me about my weight.

"You're right about one thing," I said. "Cruel remarks are

not excused by the fact that they're true. The fact that they're true is what makes them cruel."

He took my hand. I was trapped in the stinging, pinging comedown as the four martinis wore off. An electric grinder was going off in my head, some infernal factory-floor scene where I was wandering, lost, without ear protection. I'd been talking shit for the last three hours. God. Soon it would be time to eat again. And we had all day tomorrow and Sunday together.

I thought once more of Drew Gillespie, that August day in 1988, when I told him good-bye the first time: his stricken face, the pure look of hurt in his eyes.

and i got to see that look again, about an hour and a half later. Except that it was more angry than stricken. Drew was waiting for me on the steps of my apartment building. If things had proceeded normally, he would have waited all night. But I hadn't been able to stay in Marshall's bed. I was too restless.

"What if I hadn't come back here?" I said.

"You're sleeping with that guy?"

"What if I am?"
"You could have mentioned it."
"It wasn't why I called you."
"Oh, right. That was about your dad."
"Yes, it was."
"Not about this guy you're fucking."
"Come on, Drew."
"Are we just going to stand out here?"
"I don't know. I'm not sure I should ask you in."
"I am. I'm sure."

He used to be sure of everything: that we should dive into a certain rock quarry, that we should sneak up to Big Muskie, that we should shoot all the ammo we had, that we should go 140 in his Malibu SS.

"You are."

Something occurred to me, looking at him. "Are you carrying a gun, Drew?"

"What if I am?"

Turning my words back on me.

"Well, it's illegal here. Just be aware of that."
"Let's go inside."
"What for?"
"Just for a minute. I've got to tell you something. What I came to tell you. Things you need to hear."
"About my father?"
"Can we go in?"

Upstairs, I poured him a Coke. And one for myself. Trying to settle my stomach.

"You weren't in town for your dad's trial. But I went."
"Every day?"
"Not every day. But a lot of days. And no one from your family was there."

"I guess he wasn't the dad we thought we knew."

"Well, I never thought he much liked me. But seeing me at trial so often, he started to talk to me once in a while."

"Really."

"Yeah, he didn't seem to have too many friends supporting him. There really wasn't anyone but me."

I looked at his cowboy boots. They weren't familiar. They postdated me.

"Nice boots," I said.

"I could take them off."

"Tell me about the trial."

"Your father was into some wild stuff."

I thought of my dad in the backyard, shirtless, chopping wood. His white skin and his potbelly.

"I guess I wouldn't know."

"But not everything came out at the trial."

"What do you mean?"

"Well, the prosecution had a lot of evidence they never introduced. They had files and files of stuff. Well, actually, they introduced it but never referred to it. You're a lawyer. You know what I mean?"

"They entered exhibits into the record but then sort of forgot about them."

"Well, they had all these business records. Boxes of shit, and after the trial they were publicly available, if you wanted to spend the time to go through them. Well, I did."

"Really. Maybe you shouldn't be fixing cars, Drew."

"Naw. I couldn't do it if I *had* to do it, you know what I mean? If it was my job. I couldn't stand that."

"I don't blame you. I have a hard time sometimes myself."

"But it was your father. Reading about him, I was reading

about you. Every word meant something. Every number. I couldn't stop. I did it for weeks."

"Weeks? When *was* this?"

"When your dad skipped out. Your mom was packing up to go, your sisters were gone, you were gone. Home was a big hole for me. But I couldn't leave. Not the way you did."

"Once I thought I might stay."

"But you got bored."

"I guess. Hey, you didn't mention any of this the last time I saw you."

"I guess it didn't come up." He smiled at me. An insinuating smile. Fair enough, I supposed. Considering what happened the last time we met.

"What did you find out?"

"I found out some things. I found out your dad started his first sham business in 1974."

"That early."

"That's right. He was the silent partner in a bunch of real estate deals. Then in 1979 things really took off."

Nineteen seventy-nine. I was thirteen. I was walking around in a hormone haze, already boy-crazy. I wasn't keeping close tabs on my dad.

"Was that Augustine Investments?" I asked.

"Yep. And there was a partner mentioned in there, a guy who was gone by 1981. He didn't come up at the trial. He wasn't on the indictment. But it was strange. The guy'd been in Canada. I think he was a draft dodger who came back home during the Carter amnesty."

"Draft dodger? How do you know this?"

"They had your father's personal notes in this file. Stuff they'd found. Your dad referred to this guy as the draft dodger."

"What was his name?"
"The draft dodger?"
"Yes. What was his goddamn name?"
"Don't get riled up. What do you care?"
"Just tell me his name."
"Anderson or Adkinson or something. But what I wanted to tell you—"
"Atkinson? Lucius Atkinson?"
"How do you know that?"
"I know him. I work for him."
"Holy shit."
"What was it you wanted to tell me?"
"You *work* for him?"
"I do."
"Something weird here."
"No kidding."
"He ever mentioned your dad?"
"Just today he asked me about Dad. Asked me if I'd ever read *Absalom, Absalom!*"
"Have you?"
"A long time ago. I've got it right here."

I went over to my shelf of worn paperbacks and took down the novel. I knew what Lucius meant by bringing it up. My father was Thomas Sutpen. The Sutpen of Muskingum County, Ohio. I told Drew the story. Gave him a précis, the way my high school English teacher taught me to do it.

Sutpen comes to Yoknapatawpha County out of nowhere with a passel of "wild niggers," buys a hundred square miles of land from the Chickasaw Ikomotubbe in what is widely suspected by the more established residents to be a swindle of a transaction—Sutpen being the swindler here—and sets about building a plantation mansion and setting himself up as a gentleman planter. Why? We learn why, eventually. It seems that Sutpen hails from the hardscrabble mountains of Virginia, the especially hardscrabble part that later broke off to become West Virginia, and when he was a very young man, actually still in his teens, he went down to the Tidewater, to the snooty tobacco plain where the spurious aristocracy of English castoffs who'd clawed their way to precarious affluence set about extending and refining the caste snobberies of the motherland. And there the young Sutpen has what becomes the defining experience of his life: an officious servant sends him around to the back door of a house he is visiting. He never gets over this. It lights an oil fire inside him that never goes out. He spends the rest of his life putting himself into a position where he can never be sent to the back door, and in his natural power and confidence and ruthlessness he builds a minor empire. But he's not just building, he's getting even, and in getting even he destroys his family and his children and his plantation and eventually himself. He's a great dark whirlwind in the history of Yoknapatawpha County, and his descendants, decades later, and their lovers and friends, all labor in the radioactive fallout of his life. He won't go away, even in death.

"And this Atkinson told you all this?"

"No, he simply alluded to the book. I got the hint. He was telling me Dad's like the character in this book."

"He was a character, all right."

I looked at the bubbles in my Coke. Lucius had always seemed way too interested in my father.

"So what did you want to tell me about Atkinson? You were about to tell me something."

"Well, I told you your dad had a Swiss account."

"You told me that time in Central Park. I was wondering how you knew that."

"Well, it was one of the things in the first stories about the grand jury indictment. I didn't know any details then. You know, they just said things like 'illegal business interests,' 'Swiss bank accounts,' blah, blah, blah. But later I got some details. It was in some of the records. The actual account. And Atkinson was on the account, too."

"Atkinson's name was on the account? Along with my father?"

"That's what the documents said."

"Do you remember the name of the bank?"

"It had an Italian name."

"The Banca della Svizzera Italiana?"

"That sounds right."

"In Chiasso."

"I believe so."

My head was clearing now. I felt like I needed some fresh air.

"Drew, do you want to go for a walk?"

"Walk? What?"

"Do you want to take a walk?"

"I been walking. All day."

He came over and pushed my hair away from my cheek.

"Drew." Three and a half years ago: that was the last time I'd taken my clothes off for him. The last time I'd seen him. I wasn't ready for it to happen again. I stepped back away from him. He paused and looked up at me for a minute.

"I want to give you something," he said.

"What?"

"This." He handed me a business card. It was one of my father's old cards, identifying his medical practice. "Look on the back."

There was a string of numbers. It looked like sixteen or seventeen digits.

"That's his account number."

"For the Swiss account?"

"Yep. And get this: it's not the same as the one in the court papers."

"It's not?"

"It's a different one. Not the one he shared with what's-his-name."

"Atkinson."

"Atkinson. Right."

I looked at the card, ran my thumb over my father's name.

"Where did you get this?"

"Your dad gave it to me."

"He did? When?"

My heart was speeding up. It was coming on. I was getting mad again.

"The day he was convicted. He handed me the card and asked me to keep it. He said I was a good man and that he might be calling me someday."

I held the card in both hands and stared at Drew. I was about to cry. Why had my father given this card to Drew and not to me? I was jealous. And hurt. And furious.

"He never did," Drew said. "Call."

"Can I have this card?" I asked.

"I guess."

He stepped close to me and put his arms around me. The time wasn't right. I was so mad. And I was thinking of Marshall. Drew kissed me. He tried to force my teeth apart with his tongue, but I wouldn't let him in.

"What's the matter?" he asked.

"I don't know."

"I don't rate?"

"I didn't say that."

"You'll fuck him but not me?"

I jumped back and opened my apartment door.

"Go," I said.

He stood with his arms folded.

"Go on, I can't deal with you right now."

He put his hands in his back pockets and looked at me.

"No, go on. Leave. Please. This is all too much, Drew. Please. It's too much. I'll call you tomorrow."

"Where are you going to call me?"

"Where are you staying?"

"Well, I was planning on staying here. Doesn't look too promising right now."

"You can't stay here, Drew."

"You going back to loverboy? I'll have the bed to myself."

"Please. Go. You have my number. I've got to sort some stuff out. Just call me on Monday."

"Don't hold your breath."

"Come on, you can't just show up here and expect me to stop my life for you. Get real."

"You're the one who needs to get real. I'd quit that job of yours if I were you."

"Now you're giving me career advice?"

"Something's not right at that outfit."

"What do you know?"

"I know you work for a guy who used to run a scam with your dad. I just learned that. I didn't go to law school, but

I'm making better use of that information than you seem to be."

That was it. I grabbed his arm and pulled him toward the door.

"Get out of here, Drew. Thank you for coming, and thank you for the information about my dad. We'll talk on Monday."

"The hell we will. This is our last conversation."

And he was down the hall and gone.

I slammed the door and leaned against it and then tapped my forehead on the wood to try to stop crying, but that didn't work and I wept for about twenty minutes. I looked at my bed and decided there was no way I was crawling into that thing alone. It was about one in the morning. I walked out on East Capitol, dialing Marshall on my cell phone. It took him another half hour to pick me up in his Range Rover, but it was a nice night and I needed the air.

we'd been by the Dutch painters, the Hobbemas and the Hooches, and all the Impressionist frogs and the Renaissance pictures of Sebastian in ecstatic agony and Jesus the exhibitionist and the Madonna looking stoic and a bit put-upon, like a stoned Valley Girl facing her math teacher.

"No gentleman could fail to admire Bellini," Marshall had said.

Yeah yeah yeah.

An hour into our Saturday morning tour of the National Gallery and we were holding hands in front of the most bourgeois picture ever painted, Tissot's *Hide and Seek*. All my ambivalence about domestic life came flooding up. Marriage. My friend Rachel from Columbia: a mindless babbler now. Talking with her was like talking to a two-year-old. That was because you couldn't talk to her without talking to her two-year-old; no topic of conversation that might exclude the baby was permitted. Once Rachel had been an associate at Cravath. She married a partner.

"Van Zyk has been asking about you," Marshall said.

"How do you mean?"

"He wanted to be sure you'd be at the party tonight, for one thing."

Marshall was hosting a cocktail reception for the Xantex principals at his house that night. The caterers were showing up at four.

"What did you tell him?"

"That you'd be there. Of course."

"Hmmm."

"He asked me if you were seeing anyone."

"I get asked that a lot."

"I imagine. I told him I didn't know."

"What did he say to that?"

"What do you want to hear?"

"Marshall. Come on."

"I think you like him. A little."

"Maybe a little. He's such an asshole."

"I want you to be careful around him."

"Isn't he married?"

"He is. But it's irrelevant. He's always traveling, and he ruts around like a rabbit on Benzedrine."

"What are you worried about?"

"He's getting very curious about our operations. Things that are, strictly speaking, none of his business. So be on guard."

"You think I can't keep a secret?"

"You've done a good job so far."

"I've kept us a secret." I felt a pang behind my heart. Why had I told Claudia? "That hasn't been easy."

"I appreciate that. Maybe it's time we came out of the closet."

I looked back at *Hide and Seek*. He squeezed my hand.

"I don't know, Marshall. I kind of like our arrangement."

"Maybe we could take a trip."

"I wouldn't mind that."

"A long one."

"Where?"

"Laos, maybe. You said you wanted to go there."

Maybe it was time.

"I'd like to see Laos."

"Well, think about it."

"I will."

"There'll be time."

We were quiet for the rest of our tour and for most of the subway ride up to Dupont Circle. Marshall wanted to take in the Phillips, too, while we were at it. Oh, what the hell. Sure, let's stand one more time in front of *The Boating Party* while I hope one of the gallery nooks in the old building is empty so we can make out. Making out in museums is one of the true pleasures of urban life.

I was already thinking those things on the escalator at Dupont Circle, the subway entrance that most resembled the mouth of the underworld. I was in front of Marshall, a few steps up—Orpheus and Eurydice reversed. And I looked back down at him, smiling, and he smiled back, suddenly, his face all radiant beneficence, a miniature of life's most coveted possibilities. I would be stupid to let him go, I was thinking. Eurydice came into my mind, and I thought: I shouldn't have looked back. I've thought that ever since.

the office on Calvert Street had a second-story screen porch overlooking the cramped alleyway out back. I don't need to tell you how Marshall and I spent our time out there during ostensible summer night business meetings. So I won't. That afternoon after the Phillips we sat in wicker chairs while I chain-smoked and listened to him lay out the schedule for the delayed Xantex closing. An e-mail from our

London solicitors confirmed receipt of final drafts from Winslow. Things were happening without me.

"You did a great job on this," Marshall said.

I shrugged.

"No, you did."

"The truth is I never really understood this deal. I still don't know what's going on."

"Sure you do."

"I don't. The structure is wacky."

"'Innovative' is the word I would use."

"I got the feeling the contract didn't bear much relation to the actual deal."

"What do you mean?"

"I mean the Winslow contract was one thing, but the real agreement is something else."

"I don't follow you."

"Marshall."

He started doing push-ups, a holdover habit from his military days.

"Marshall."

"We called this the front lean-and-rest position. Isn't that great? The D.I.s' would go, 'Fuck the ground, boy! Fuck the ground!'"

"Marshall. The Banca della Svizzera Italiana. Did you know my father had an account there?"

"What?"

"I know that Lucius and my father used to have some secret business connection. Did you know that?"

He stopped at the top of a push-up and stared at me. I have to say, he looked genuinely surprised.

"That sounds a little far-fetched to me."

"That's news to you?"

"Where did you hear that? From Lucius?"

"A little bird."

He resumed his push-ups, more slowly now.

"Have you been lying to me, sweetheart?" I asked.

No answer. I counted thirty, thirty-five, forty.

"Lucius never said anything to you, Marshall?"

"He said you were smarter than you looked." He finished his set of push-ups and rocked back on his knees, huffing.

I blew smoke rings and glared.

"He was right," Marshall said.

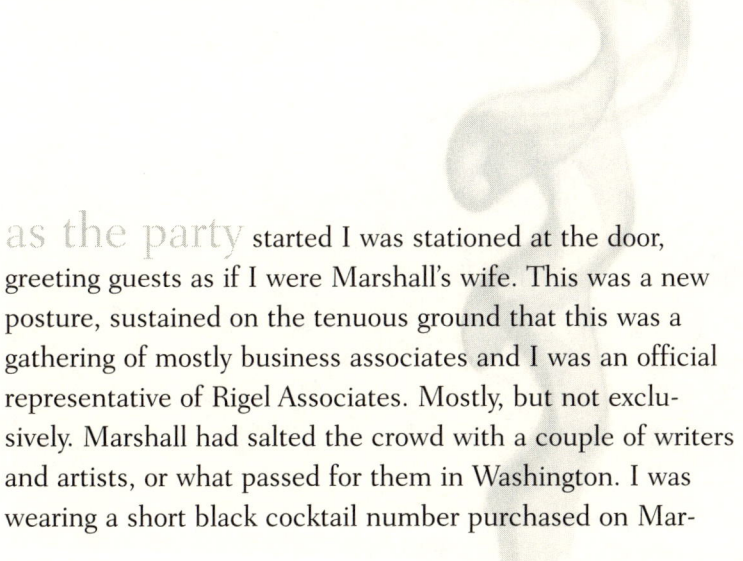

as the party started I was stationed at the door, greeting guests as if I were Marshall's wife. This was a new posture, sustained on the tenuous ground that this was a gathering of mostly business associates and I was an official representative of Rigel Associates. Mostly, but not exclusively. Marshall had salted the crowd with a couple of writers and artists, or what passed for them in Washington. I was wearing a short black cocktail number purchased on Marshall's tab, and in spite of the visible flesh overload at my waistline I must say I did look great. The head-snaps and the sidewise stares I registered out of the corner of my paint-doctored eyes confirmed my self-assessment. I was on tonight. Luxury vibes washed over me, and I thought: I could get used to this. I could grow into this. It was only after an hour or so that creeping disgust—the bane of my life—started to take the edge off the fun and drove me to the bar in search of a third drink. Deep inside me lived an outraged nun.

"Some real characters here tonight," Lucius said. He was holding a vodka martini and wearing a collarless shirt. Of course he's gay, I thought.

"You mean the South Africans? They're your friends."

"Clients."

"Clients, then."

"Van Zyk asked me about you."

"Oh, really. You, too."

"He'll be here shortly."

"I can't wait."

"Does he bore you, too?"

"Intermittently."

"Ask him about the Jews sometime."

"I don't want to know."

"Did you know that the runways at Heathrow, seen from the air, form a Star of David?"

"Get out of here. And you actually do business with this guy?"

"A lot of business."

"Heathrow. I guess he's flown into London one too many times."

"Evidently. Perfidious Albion, you know."

I didn't know, but I let it go. "Good grub tonight."

"Have you tried the phyllo doodads?"

I had but said I hadn't.

"They're good. Curried chicken and walnuts. Try one."

I tried three. Lucius attacked when my mouth was full.

"You eat, therefore you are," he said. "And thus you refute Berkeley."

I didn't get it, but I could tell it was insulting. One of those Venus of Willendorf things. His back was turned by the time I swallowed and emitted my "Fuck you."

Asshole.

And speaking of which, in came Van Zyk. He wasted no time making right for me, and I gave him my brightest smile.

"Roos!" I burbled, in full tart mode.

"Rosalind, darling," he said, kissing me on the cheek. The mule farmer was suddenly Dirk Bogarde. A dark scene flashed in my head, sunglasses at midnight. "I was hoping I'd see you here."

"Well, here I am."

"So you are."

"So she is," Lucius said, turning to join us. I clamped my teeth together, just keeping my tongue from poking out at him. I gave Roos my smile again.

"Are you enjoying Washington?"

"As much as business permits."

"Well, what have you seen?"

"The Hotel Washington roof!" He laughed, a big Afrikaner cackle. Lucius, laughing along, raised his glass in salute.

"It's the only thing in Washington worth visiting," I said. "So have you been drinking all day?"

"I have."

"Don't stop on my account."

"I don't intend to."

The bartender handed him two whiskeys.

"You're drinking two at once?" I asked.

"One's for you."

"Actually, I was in the mood for a gin and tonic."

"Take the whiskey."

I did. And then Marshall finally joined us. He introduced us to Harvey Gitlin, one of his writer guests. Thin and intense. Trimmed black beard. I'd heard of Harvey. He'd made a big splash with a book on moral philosophy. He was an upscale version of Pat Robertson, an intellectual who decried American moral decay. Of course, he himself had no intention of giving up arugula salads or anal intercourse or any of the other joys of urban life, but he correctly understood that if the whole country is Greenwich Village, Greenwich Village loses its point. You've got to have Peoria, or Adams-Morgan is a senseless exercise.

"How can you call yourself a conservative and still praise the free market?" That was Lucius. Uh-oh. The old Columbia soapboxer died hard. Poor Gitlin looked at me. I fed him a phyllo triangle. He liked that. He didn't get to see the likes of me on the right-wing academic circuit.

"There's nothing more revolutionary," Lucius went on, "more continuously destructive to traditions, than the free market. What do you say to that?"

"Well, of course, as a practical matter, we want a mixed economy."

"Yes. Privatize gains, socialize losses."

I took Harvey's arm and drew him away from the group.

He was quite willing. My heart warmed at Van Zyk's drooping look of disappointment. The whole scene was a throwback to one of my school hobbies, which was making smart boys lose control of themselves. I was very good at it.

"Don't pay any attention to Lucius," I said. "He's a capitalist pig himself, and in no position to talk." Though I thought Lucius had a point. Righteousness does poorly on the free market. Offered sin, people choose it. They have to be coerced into behaving better. That's what the Catholic Church always understood.

"A real capitalist pig, eh?"

"The real thing."

"What do you do?"

"I'm his lawyer."

"Really. How interesting."

"It can be. Most of the time it's not."

"You don't look like a lawyer. I mean that as a compliment."

"And that's how I'll take it."

I was edging him around the hors d'oeuvres table, because I had a craving for some of the cold shrimp. But I wanted Marshall and Lucius and Van Zyk to see me laughing with this guy, not maneuvering into position to stuff my face again. So I was keeping my back to the food. I could feel the shrimp, though. I knew where they were without looking.

"What are you writing now?" I asked.

"An analysis of American higher education."

"That must be a hoot."

"'Hoot' is the word."

"Have you tried the shrimp?"

"No, I haven't."

"Have some." I fed him again, letting my fingers linger on his lips just a half-second. Van Zyk would have licked them. Harvey was a tad shy. "This is a diverse table."

"Diversity," Harvey said. "Watchword of the times."

"Isn't it, though?"

"Diversity is the latest euphemism for mediocrity in the academy. Its predecessor was relevance."

"The inmates have taken over the asylum." Now I was facing the table. I did the shrimp thing. I put down four or five cheese balls while Harvey ran through his rap.

"We're an international joke . . . the undergraduate experience in this country . . . it's a scandal . . . the end of meaningful distinctions . . . the dictatorship of the ignorant . . . that's the future."

Amen, brother. I was zeroing in on the sausage pinwheels—one good thing about the testosterone world of investment banking, you don't have to endure vegetarian buffets—and remembering my own days in the academy. Pizza, and lots of it. That's what being an undergraduate was all about.

Our move down the table brought us back to Lucius. I fucked up. My mouth was full again.

"Yes, we're a nation of whiners," Lucius said. "Everybody's got their little cause. We've all been to college, dipped our toes in the Pierian spring. What can we do about it, Harvey?"

I finally swallowed and cleared my throat.

"What this country needs is a collective vow of silence." I looked at Lucius as I said this. "Things would get better fast." Then I winked at Harvey.

An arm circled around me from behind, entering my field

of vision from the left. The big hand at the end of the arm held another whiskey.

"For you," Van Zyk murmured in my ear.

I took the drink and turned to face him.

"Why, thank you, sir."

Now it was Harvey with the drooping expression.

"I flew from Johannesburg especially to see you."

"You flew from Johannesburg to attend the Xantex closing."

"I didn't have to be here."

"Sure you did."

"No. Could have sent a proxy. Wanted to see you in person."

Now I was thinking. *Could have sent a proxy. Probably could have.* That Winslow agreement was a shadow document. Who cared who signed it?

"So, Roos, how's your wife?"

"Busy with her own life."

"The kids?"

"Living with my first wife."

"I see."

"What are you doing later?"

"I'm going to bed."

"Yes. But with whom?"

"You naughty boy. None of your business."

"With that Hebrew thinker of deep thoughts, perhaps?"

"Roos, five minutes ago you were doing all right. But you've seriously blown it. Now, if you'll excuse me—"

"And if I don't excuse you?"

But I was already gone, heading for the safe haven of Marshall. I wanted to fall all over him, but that would have been inappropriate. As they say. We hadn't come out of the closet. Of course, not being able to grab him made the urge almost irresistible. I stood close as he chatted with a middle-aged woman I didn't know. Pretending to whisper to him, I teased an earlobe with the tip of my tongue.

"Rosalind, have you met Rhonda Blake?"

"No. How do you do?"

She was a Corcoran trustee. Marshall knew such people. After a short exchange of niceties, I managed to pull Marshall aside. I whispered in his ear.

"I think I maybe pissed off Van Zyk."

"Good for you."

"Is that a problem? For the deal?"

"The deal is done. Wild horses couldn't change it."

"He's after me."

"Yes."

We looked back across the room.

"Actually, he doesn't look very pissed to me," Marshall said. "He's coming this way."

And so he was. With Lucius and Harvey Gitlin in tow. Offered me a gin and tonic. "A peace offering," he said. "Let me apologize for my behavior."

"All right."

"I should have gotten you a gin and tonic the first time."

"But you're a quick study."

"That he is," Lucius said.

"Lucius, I need to talk to you sometime," I said.

"Why not now?"

"Not here. On Monday."

"Something important?"

"I think so. Yes."

"On Monday, then."

I don't think I'm easily shocked, but I was certainly startled by what happened next. Lucius put his arm around me, more than casually, and with his right hand fondly manipulated my deltoid. Lucius who'd never actually touched me before. Maybe he wasn't a screamer, after all. What was going on here?

"Harvey thinks our American pop-culture infatuation with transvestites is an example of pernicious European influence," Lucius said. "And Roos says that Europe has nothing to do with it. He says decadence follows affluence. It has no pedigree."

He'd pushed a button with me. As much as I wanted to smile and look down on them all from a stance of Olympian detachment, I'd had it with the whole drag queen deal.

"It's just misogyny," I said. "It's a P.C. way to hate women. A structural hatred that's completely institutionalized and shielded by our reverence for gay culture. It makes me sick."

I needed to shut up. Part of me knew that, but the rest of me was drunk. And Lucius's grip on me got tighter. I relaxed against him, mostly out of curiosity. Where was this going?

"That's a very interesting view," Harvey said. "I'd like to discuss it with you sometime."

Oh, come on, Harvey, I very nearly said. *That's up there with "Look at my etchings."*

"Use it in your next book," is what I did say.

"I might do that."

"The man writes books," Roos said. I recognized the tone. A suitor, simultaneously assessing and dismissing a rival.

"He wrote one called *The Therapeutic Delusion,*" Lucius said, addressing me. "Ever read it?"

"Heard of it," I said. "Never read it. What's it about?"

"Art," said Harvey.

"Art, culture, politics," Lucius said. "Harvey hit all the bases." I detected the same submerged belligerence that emanated from Van Zyk. What an inspiration I was. Even Lucius had thrown his hat in the ring.

"America drains life of tragedy," Harvey intoned. "That's all I was saying. And we drain our art the same way. Art isn't therapy. Art isn't good for you. This country can't face that."

"You're channeling George Steiner," Lucius said. He grinned at me and Van Zyk. "He's the North American discount outlet for George Steiner."

That was enough. Time to level the playing field. I detached myself from Lucius and attached myself to Harvey. I'd give him another shot here. I whispered in his ear: "I love George Steiner." Memo to myself: look up George Steiner. Heard the name, never read the books.

"How did you end up in corporate law?" Harvey appeared genuinely puzzled.

"Path of least resistance."

"It's amazing how the most boring occupations have become fashionable."

"It's money," Lucius said. "Money isn't boring. People are finally admitting that making money is the most interesting thing you can do."

"I'd take issue with that," Harvey said. Poor boy.

"You would," said Van Zyk.

"Yes, I would."

"Because you're outside looking in. But you'd love to dive into a hundred million dollars."

"Like Scrooge McDuck," I said.

"There's no feeling like it," said Van Zyk.

"I'll have to take your word for that," Harvey said.

I slipped my card into the inside pocket of Harvey's jacket.

"Call me," I'd written on it.

Harvey brought up South Africa. I almost took my card back. Van Zyk was cool now. His positions were moderate, unprovocative. Lucius, like Van Zyk, seemed to be drawing into himself. His strange paroxysm of heterosexual bonhomie appeared to have passed.

"Are we having fun now?" Marshall asked.

My five drinks had me a little dizzy, and I sprawled on the sofa, surveying the room. My aspiring suitors were ranged in a row, talking to each other and throwing glances at me. I realized that I was the only woman in the room visible to them. Men have that radar, that pitiless binary female assessor that tells them yes or no with just a second's worth of visual input. The gooniest twerp has the damn thing, and either you register on it or you don't. My sisters and I would sit around the dinner table, watching my dad chew his food and stare at the wall over our heads, and we were all thinking, Look at *me*, Look at *me*, Look at *me*. But since then plenty of other men had taken up the slack. I knew, of course, that the time would come when men would stop looking at me and start looking through me. That my favorite hobby and pastime would no longer be available to me.

So.

So I'd spend more time practicing my mandolin.

That time hadn't come yet.

"Happy Halloween." Van Zyk had found a ghoul mask somewhere. He was standing over me, his face a bloody skull. Seeing him made me think about South African laws governing structured finance. Behind all those measured words, behind all those reasonable regulations, all the centuries of common-law contract interpretation, guarantees, and assignment of rights, there was only this—a bloody skull. It seemed I was seeing the world whole. The distilled truth. But then again I was drunk.

"Happy Halloween," I answered. "What we say here is 'Trick or treat?'"

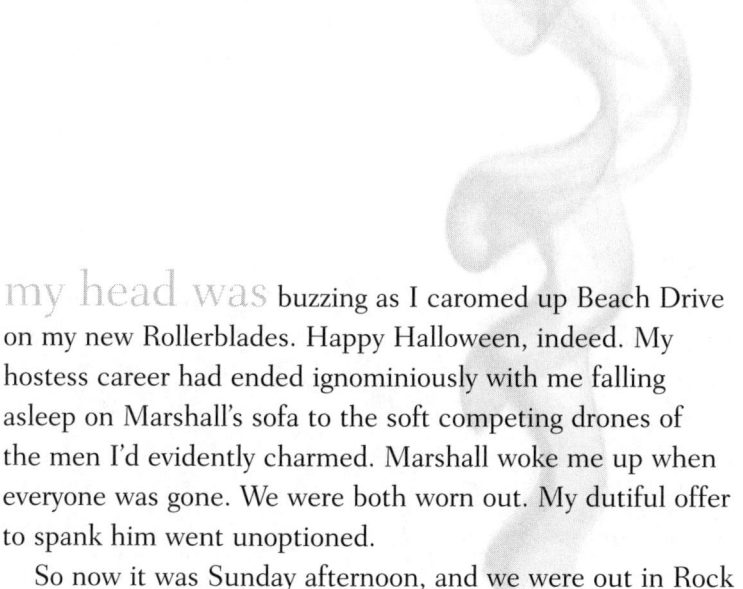

my head was buzzing as I caromed up Beach Drive on my new Rollerblades. Happy Halloween, indeed. My hostess career had ended ignominiously with me falling asleep on Marshall's sofa to the soft competing drones of the men I'd evidently charmed. Marshall woke me up when everyone was gone. We were both worn out. My dutiful offer to spank him went unoptioned.

So now it was Sunday afternoon, and we were out in Rock

Creek Park, getting some exercise. Marshall was surprisingly good on skates, yet another way he avoided old-fart status. I was looking at his trim rear end, certainly trimmer than mine, as I worked to stay in visual range. For me it was a matter of wind. I was just plain out of shape. It wasn't a matter of balance or skill. I was a good skater. Back in my Ohio youth I'd grown up on ice skates. My happiest memory is of myself and my sisters out on a frozen pond, for hours and hours, playing our improvised games, weaving arabesques on the ice, unrestrainedly yelling for joy.

No yelling this day. Not from me, anyway. I was, of course, drawing stares. I should have been happy, a yuppie wonder, whizzing along behind my rich lover on this road closed to cars and full of admiring athletic men. But I was saddled with a headache. Too much drink, and too much suppressed tension. Xantex. The fly in the soup. And this business of Lucius and my father. I looked at the fall foliage, at the drifting roadside leaves, and I reflected that autumn—season of death—was always my favorite season. I think it's because of the academic cycle: we don't grow up with the rhythms of the earth but with the rhythms of school, and fall—not spring—is the time of renewal, of stainless new beginnings. My annual promises to improve come on Labor Day, not New Year's Eve.

Rock Creek Park is the biggest urban park I've ever seen. It's not like Central Park, where beyond the trees you can always see the towers you could never afford to live in. No. Rock Creek Park looks like the hills of North Carolina. If it weren't for all the spandex on the roads and the Saab-Subaru overload in the parking lots, you might think you were *in* North Carolina. You can't see the city from here. You can only sense it, looking at the suspicious bubbles in the creek.

Marshall disappeared around a bend, and I struggled to close the gap between us. I thought of him smiling up at me on the escalator at Dupont Circle. Mother would be so happy if I just called and said I'm getting married, I'm joining my sisters on Planet Volvo. And I couldn't blame her. She just wanted to see me settled, so she could relax. I'd always been her problem child. She wasn't pleased when I left Winslow to take this job at Rigel Associates. She thought I was being flip and cavalier again, even though I was still making plenty of money. And there'd been a suspiciously long stretch when I'd brought no man home to meet her, or even alluded to a boyfriend. There were plenty who wanted to come. I just couldn't bring myself to invite them. And now there was Marshall. Would I be introducing him to my family at Thanksgiving?

   A young couple occupied the roadway in front of me, bending over their designer stroller and cooing at their baby. The stroller looked like you could enter it in the Baja 1000, so fat were the tires and so elaborate was the coil spring suspension. They were lawyers. I could smell it. That would be me in a couple of years. Only they'd never stood in a strip mine, and their fathers had never been indicted. Part of me hated those people. Part of me always will.

why get up?

That was the first question of the day, one I managed to table in favor of considering the alternative: what time do I have to be at work?

Even that question was not cut-and-dried. I'd learned that much at law school. No, it was subject to boundless interpretation, swathed in deep layers of encrusted if perhaps outmoded association that demanded to be vigorously deconstructed. And such deconstruction was what I, from a wide spread-eagle in the enfolding warmth of my downy covers, was eminently capable of supplying. It seemed to me that the start of the workday is like the location of an electron in the quantum mechanical universe: not a fixed point, but a constellation of probabilities. Thinking of a fixed point is not even the right way to think. So it is with the start of the workday.

I was back in my own apartment, in my own bed. Marshall had dropped me off here after our afternoon in the park. "Get some sleep," he'd said. "I'll see you at the office." We'd kissed. Like married people. Decorous. No tongue work. I liked it and I didn't like it. My anxiety about that kiss was linked with my approaching thirty-third birthday. The future: decorous and no tongue work. That was the problem with being an adult.

The phone rang. The clock said 6:59. I reached for the receiver.

"Hello."

"Hey, Rosalind, it's Lucius."

Lucius. He'd never called me at home. He'd faxed but never called.

"Hey, hippie peacenik." I steeled myself for the tongue-free future.

"I'm sorry to bother you at this hour."

"It's okay."

"Listen. I just got a call from the police."

"What about?"

I once lost control of my car—my little MG—on the freeway in Atlanta, and I spun across three lanes of high-speed traffic before miraculously coming to rest on the shoulder. I had a strange sensation of detachment, of being suspended over an abyss, knowing I was going to die but very resigned to it. I had, in the moment before Lucius's next words, the same fleeting sensation.

"Marshall's dead."

I knew that. Or something like that. That's why I said, "Hey, hippie peacenik." Something inside me knew it was my last chance.

"Oh. Oh. Oh, no."

"He shot himself. Or that's what they're saying now, anyway."

"When?"

"Last night, they think."

"I was with him yesterday."

"I know."

He knew. What else did he know? Everything, probably.

"Marshall wouldn't shoot himself," I said.

"Did you two have a fight?"

"Fight? No. About what?"

"I don't know."

"How about you? Did you have a fight?"

"Listen, you'd better get in here. We need to talk."

Of course, that's what I said to him at the party Saturday night. And I was committing the same sin of avoiding the point. I think the four words anyone most dreads are "We need to talk." Just get to the "You have inoperable rectal cancer," I say. Don't bother telling me we need to talk.

I hung up and looked around my apartment. The same fucking mess. But I wanted to savor it, in all its postcollegiate innocence, before I walked out into my new life.

when i got to the office, Claudia was crying. The Australian receptionist had been her crisp self, but Claudia was a wreck. I was still dry-eyed. That would change, in time.

"I can't believe it," she said.
"Has anyone been here this morning?" I asked.
"Anyone . . . who do you mean?"
"Any clients? Any police?"

"Not yet."
"Not yet?"
"The police are coming."
"You know that?"
"They called."
"Lucius is waiting to see me."
"Does he know?"
"Know what?"
"That you were seeing Marshall."
"Probably."
"Yeah."
"I think he knows everything."
"I can't believe he killed himself. Why?"
"I don't know. I can't believe it, either."

She took a phone call, sniffling. I walked across the hall to Lucius's office. He was on the phone, too, but he motioned me to sit down.

"We're going to do the deal," he was saying. "There may be a short delay, but we'll close. Soon." He looked at me, then rolled his eyes.

Xantex? I silently mouthed.

He held up an admonishing finger. *Shut up,* the finger said.

I was already getting ticked off with him.

I couldn't believe he was on the phone blowing off the news about his dead partner as a minor inconvenience, a "short delay" in the almighty closing schedule.

"I can't believe you," I said when he finally hung up.

"Life goes on."

"Jesus Christ."

"I need you to get with Winslow and get the Xantex closing back on track. We're still under pressure there."

"Aren't you going to tell me how sorry you are about Marshall?"

"It's enormously inconvenient, yes. His timing was terrible."

"You really think he killed himself?"

"I presume. It's not entirely implausible. We've had a couple of deals go south. He could have been depressed."

"He didn't seem particularly depressed to me."

"And you saw a side of him the rest of us didn't, isn't that right?"

"Okay, Lucius, let's just get it all out in the open."

He surprised me by slamming his hand down on his desk.

"This is all your fault, Rosalind."

"What?"

"All your fault. You inspired Marshall. You fucked up his mind. He lost it. He lost it because of you."

"What the hell? I can't believe I'm hearing this."

"He started thinking he wanted a different life. A life with you. He lost his nerve. He decided he wanted to pull out of the game. There was only one way to do that."

"Leave me out of this."

"Way too late for that. And the funny thing is, he didn't really want to hire you. We argued about it. We had the story on you. Eric Hoffman told me all about you."

"I can imagine. So did he tell you I wouldn't fuck him?"

"He said you were like a sex grenade. That you threw the office into an uproar and nobody could get any work done."

"I didn't do anything. That pathetic liar."

"It's what you made them want to do to you."

"Now you're being sexist."

"No, I'm not. You know what I'm talking about."

Of course I did. And so what? Tough shit. *Are you really a fag?* is what I didn't say. "At least they were alive for a few minutes," I did say. "It was a novel experience for them."

"Eric stayed up at night," Lucius said, "thinking of you."

I didn't want to stoop to this, but when men start fighting dirty, you have to respond in kind. Fire with fire.

"Well, I have it on good authority that he has trouble performing. I never slept with him, but I know women who did. How do you think he got his nickname? Super Wiener. It was one of those ironic monikers. Drooper Wiener was more like it."

"You're such a bitch."

"Do you blame me?"

He tucked his chin into his chest and grabbed his thinning hair with both fists.

"And anyway," I said, "why did you hire me? Who put Hoffman up to bringing me that *American Lawyer* ad? Huh? I might never have seen it. And I might never have answered it. But you wanted me here, for some reason."

"What had he told you?"

"Who?"

"Marshall."

"About what?"

"Anything."

"He didn't tell me that you and my father used to be business partners. I found that out on my own."

He quit grabbing his hair and stared at me.

"You want to tell me about that, Lucius?"

"Marshall didn't know about that."

"He had to know."

"He didn't, actually. It was before I linked up with him. But that was the connection. It was how I met the man who brought us together."

"Was this at the urinal?"

"No, not exactly."

"Are you saying Marshall didn't know my father?"

"He didn't know about my connection to your father. Arlie introduced us. I'd stopped working with your dad. But I was still running his money. The Augustine money. Marshall just knew it as Augustine money. He didn't ask where every nickel and dime in the Xantex investment account came from."

I sat down. "Let's have it. Just lay it on me now."

"What did Marshall tell you about his dealings with the FBI?"

"He told me about a guy named Arlie Ralston. And a guy named Trevor something."

"Langford."

"That's right."

"What did he say about Trevor?"

"He was trying to take over a bank."

"That's right. Anything else?"

"Not really. What else is there?"

"Trevor Langford introduced me to Marshall."

"Okay."

"We're both in a lot of trouble, Rosalind."

"No. I'm not in trouble. You might be."

"You spent Sunday with Marshall."

"Only the afternoon."

"You were rollerblading in the park."

"How did you know that?"

"Marshall told me on Saturday that he would be blading on Sunday."

"With me?"

"He left that part out."

"But you knew."

"I knew."

"How long?"

"How long what?"

"How long have you known about me and Marshall?"

The phone rang. He let the voice mail handle it.

"A while. What time did you leave his house?"

"I didn't. He drove me straight home from the park. It was around five."

"You'd spent the night with him."

"I was co-located with him in his bed. That was the extent of our interaction."

"But you were lovers. On most other occasions."

"Is that your business?"

"I'm afraid it is. Now it is."

"This whole operation is a front, isn't it?"

He turned his back to me and tapped his keyboard.

"The whole thing is a fake." My temper was surging. "All these deals, all these contracts, all bullshit. My whole job is a charade. Who really funds this operation?"

He turned back.

"Rosalind, these next few days are crucial. I need you to ride herd on this Xantex closing. We've got to get through that. I have no one else I can count on."

"You can't count on me."

"I'm going to have to explain something to you. Something about your father."

"I was just going to ask about that."

"It's difficult."

"Let's just start at the beginning. Nineteen seventy-nine."

"You're really something."

"So I've been told."

"Where did you get that date, 1979?"

"It's not right?"

The intercom buzzed. It was the Australian receptionist.

"Mr. Atkinson. The police are here."

"Thank you," Lucius said. "We'll be right down."

"It's right," he said to me. "Please, just for now, let's be friends."

it wasn't just the police, as it turned out. There was an FBI man, too. Gregory Payson.

"Call me Greg."

We were sitting in the small first-floor conference room. Just me and Greg. Balding, earnest Greg. Kept himself in shape, I could see that. Wedding ring. Family man. He looked at me the way family men tended to look at me: like I was a reminder of something they missed.

"Hello, Greg."

"Hello. Well, I'm sorry to have to talk to you about all this. I know you must be grieving."

"And why is that?"

The local cops had not assumed I was grieving. I'd given them the facts as I technically interpreted them: Marshall and I were employer and employee, and beyond that, "just friends"; I had no idea why he might want to kill himself; he was fine when I last saw him. Yes, I'd call if anything else occurred to me.

But then there was Greg. And my flip response—"Why is that?"—I could already see was a mistake. Of course I should have been grieving. And I was, in my own way. But I felt awkward about my secret relationship with Marshall. So awkward I couldn't acceptably emote for this particular audience.

"Are you denying you had a romantic relationship with the deceased?"

What was the big deal? And how did everybody know? I felt like asking to have an attorney present—someone besides myself—and to stop answering questions, but then it looks like you're guilty of something. That's how they get people to talk during these informal interviews. It seems churlish and incriminating to refuse.

"All right, we had a romantic relationship."

"And how long had this been going on?"

"Almost a year."

"When did you start work at Rigel Associates?"

"August of '98."

"Where did you work before that?"

"In the New York office of Winslow, Cooper, and Stowe."

"That's a law firm?"

"That's right."

"How long did you work there?"

"Almost five years. I started in September of '93."

"Right out of law school?"

"Well, almost. I'd spent a year getting an LL.M."

He studied his notes. The window behind him faced diagonally across Constitution Avenue. It was divided into many small panes, like a checkerboard. I looked across the broad intersection at the facade of the Sewall-Belmont House.

"Can you tell me something about the work you do here?"

"Here? I'm the general counsel."

"And what does that entail?"

"A lot."

He pursed his lips to convey dissatisfaction.

"For example?"

"I oversee the documentation for the transactions we do. Documenting deals. That's basically what I do. The outside law firms draft documents, and I review and approve them. That's most of it."

"So you have a good idea of the scope of the firm's activities."

"I would hope so."

"Do you get involved in putting deals together?"

"Sometimes."

"How so?"

"Usually I'm part of the negotiations with the client. I advise on how a deal should be structured."

"Were you responsible, are you responsible, for dealing with Xantex, Inc.?"

Ahh, shit.

"What does this have to do with Marshall Waverly's suicide?"

"I don't know. I'm trying to find out. I'm hoping you can help me."

"What are you investigating here?"

"I've been dealing with Mr. Waverly on a number of matters. He was cooperating with me. Now he's dead, and I'm just trying to learn everything I can about what he was doing."

Dealing with Mr. Waverly. Like, for a while now. Like, during our romance. Uh-oh.

"He was doing project finance deals, as far as I'm aware."

"Yes. I presume you keep files."

"Of course I keep files."

"And those files would reflect all the firm activity in which you are involved."

"Yes."

"Do you recall any firm dealings with a man named Trevor Langford?"

"No."

"Would you necessarily recall everyone the firm has dealt with?"

"No."

"That's what I thought. Have you heard of Mr. Langford?"

"I've heard the name."

"Waverly mentioned it?"

"He did. Once."

"When?"

"Recently."

"How recently."

"Friday afternoon."

"You specifically remember it was Friday afternoon."

"Yes."

"Why?"

I'd already had it with this guy. Unlike a boyfriend, I couldn't just tell him to shut up and hit the road. I had to try and be nice. It was a challenge I wasn't sure I could meet.

"It was Friday afternoon."

"All right."

I looked out the window, wishing I could just walk away.

"Now, about Xantex."

"Yes."

"You didn't answer my question."

"Which was?"

"Are you responsible for any or all aspects of the firm's dealings with Xantex."

"I have some responsibility. I don't think I have the big picture, necessarily. I see documents. I see details."

"God is in the details, someone said."

I kept my mouth shut.

"When you say you don't have the big picture, does that mean that things go on around here without your knowledge?"

"That's possible."

"Is it what you believe?"

"I don't know. What are you getting at?"

"Miss Wilcox, have you ever observed any activity on these premises that you knew to be illegal?"

"No, I have not."

"Thank you. We'll talk again."

Of that I had no doubt.

"so what did you tell him?"

Lucius was throwing sticks of gum into his mouth. He was back on the barricades. The ghettos were burning. The cops were on their way to rescue the dean.

"Not much. I don't know much. What did you tell him?"

"The little prick. A Mormon. Half the FBI is Mormon. And this guy. You didn't want to be in the way when his psychotic forebears overran the state of Utah and set up their cult fiefdom. It's the same thing now. Don't get in their fucking way."

"Well, he has God on his side."

"God the functionary. A God wearing Hush Puppies and a pocket protector."

"Yeah, well. There's no one more boring than the village atheist."

"I never said I was an atheist. But Christianity is an unacceptable domestication of the numinous."

"And what is Wall Street?"

He shoved another stick of gum into his mouth. "Never mind. You're distracting me. What did you say to the pious bastard?"

"Regarding what?"

"Regarding Xantex."

"It's all about Xantex, isn't it? I didn't tell him anything, because I don't know anything. The only thing I know is that four million dollars disappeared from the escrow account, and no one will tell me where it went."

"You said that?"

"I did not say that. But I will."

"No, you won't."

He spoke quietly.

"Your father has that money," he said.

"That's crazy."

"You wanted to know the story. I'm ready to share."

"I'm listening."

"Well, it all started with Jimmy Carter."

"President Carter."

"He declared an amnesty for draft evaders."

"He let you back in the States."

"He let me come home."

"Just another of his many, many mistakes."

"I suppose. You were a baby when Carter was president."

"I was ten years old. Fourteen when Ronnie came in to restore order."

"I came back across the border in 1978. My father died and I had some money coming. I was looking for a good way to invest it. I was looking to get back on my feet. In Toronto I'd met a man named Trevor Langford. A Brit."

"Our man Trevor."

"Our man. Had his fingers in many a pie. He had an idea. He thought there might be a market for retail-level money laundering. A way to connect small dirty operators to large legitimate institutional investors. To pool and commingle their funds, get the money working in legal investments. What he needed was a vehicle. A boutique investment firm with Wall Street links to the big houses."

"Rigel Associates."

"Well, eventually. That was later. That was what Marshall brought to the table. The links to legitimacy."

"He was at First Boston."

"He was known and respected."

"Why would he get involved in this?"

"Why does anyone get involved in this?"

"Money."

"You sound disappointed."

"I am."

"Well, Marshall was an idiot. And you're the proof."

"I'm not going to listen to this."

"I think you are. We're coming to your father. You don't want to hear it?"

"All right. I'm listening."

"I was in Cleveland, checking things out, and I got a tip. An investment opportunity. There was this outfit, Augustine Investments. Out of podunk Zanesville. They had an unreported interest in properties in Columbus, in Pittsburgh, in Cleveland, in Wheeling, in Morgantown, West Virginia. Oh, it was a going concern. And I hung around and dangled money that Trevor fronted me, and eventually I met your dad. Never in Zanesville. First time was in Cleveland."

"You didn't live in Zanesville?"

"Of course not. I lived in New York."

"Oh, yeah? Where?"

"Inwood."

"Huh."

"Spent a lot of time at the Cloisters."

"Didn't take, did it?"

"Once I hooked up with Marshall, and we set up Rigel Associates, I went back and offered your father a conduit into the investment pool. It was all supposed to be offshore, but we set up a Cayman Islands account, and everything went through that."

"How much are we talking about?"

"Well, not much in the grand scheme. I mean, once the South African money started coming in big, and once we started piggybacking the big firms on their legitimate deals, it wasn't significant at all. In fact I sort of forgot about the whole thing. Until he disappeared, and we suddenly needed to talk to him."

"About what?"

"About a certain Swiss account."

"At the Banca Italiana."

"That's right."

"I bet I know this part."

"We were hoping maybe he would stay in touch with you and that maybe we could locate him through you."

"Why?"

"Well, there were disputed sums. He kept some money that we thought was legitimately part of our fee. That wasn't such a big deal. And this is partly my fault. I mean through laziness or sloppiness I just really fucked up. The Xantex escrow account . . ."

"Yeah?"

"I shouldn't go into it."

"Oh, I think you should."

"Van Zyk blames me."

"Sounds like he has good reason."

"He wants me to restore the four million."

"You, personally?"

"He says it was my fuckup."

"Was it?"

"I suppose."

"My father stole the money in the account?"

"He moved it."

"How could he do that?"

"It goes back to the business in 1979."

"The joint account."

"You know about that?"

"News flash, Lucius: that account is a matter of public record. It was evidence considered by the grand jury that indicted my father."

"I didn't know that. And I didn't know you knew that. When did you learn all this?"

"You had a joint account, and you were so stupid you never closed it. You just started using it as the Xantex escrow account."

"Not my finest hour. Answer my question."

"Don't ever call me an idiot again, Lucius."

"Okay. You're not an idiot."

"And neither was Marshall."

"Well, I think that's debatable. So when did you find out that I knew your father?"

"Recently."

"And how?"

"I'll say what I told Marshall. A little bird."

"All right. We all have our little secrets."

"So about the escrow account."

"Your father—I'm sure of this—moved that missing four million to another account at the same bank. He did it just a month ago. Sometime in that week before we found it gone. You found it gone."

"Jesus."

"So now there is a very urgent desire in certain circles to locate your father."

"You mean *you* want to locate my father."

"Well, yes I do. This four million is not the first time. Your father stole two million when he disappeared back in '94."

"From this same account? And you didn't do anything about it?"

"No, it's money he just took with him."

"How did he get it?"

"I can't go into it right now. The point is, Van Zyk thinks I stole his money. I haven't told him yet about your father. Do you want me to?"

"I'm not my father's keeper."

"You really don't know where he is?"

"You know I don't."

"Yes, I believe you. But Van Zyk won't. And that's why I say that you and I are both in trouble. Not with the FBI. With Van Zyk."

"You'd sic Van Zyk on me just to get him off your back?"

"I didn't say that."

"You can't save yourself here. The cops are onto you."

"I'm not worried about the cops. I'm worried about my chief client."

"Let's just turn him in."

"Marshall already did that. They want more."

"Marshall did . . . what?"

"I think Marshall was talking to the cops."

"And I'm going to take up where he left off," I said.

"You going to give them your father?"

"You know I don't know where he is."

"They won't believe you."

"What is your point?"

"We can put this all off on Van Zyk. As far as we're concerned, we were doing a straight-up project finance deal."

"And the missing money?"

"It's not missing."

"What, you wrote a personal check?"

"The feds aren't going to know about the missing four million."

"Why not?"

"Because the money is in a new account," Lucius said. "Here's the number. Go look."

"The money was gone, but now it's back." I shrugged my shoulders, gave him a quizzical "What gives?" look.

"Well, it's not the same money. The four million is gone,

but we're going to gloss over that small inconvenience, for now."

"What's the cover story?"

"We shifted it to cover some contingencies on another deal. That wasn't strictly kosher, but it's also no big whoop. It's something that would be awkward to explain, but you know it's just something we do all the time."

"That's our story?"

"Hey, you know, it's sometimes the truth."

"But usually I know about it."

"Yeah, well, I'm sorry. I'll keep you informed from here on out."

That was the baldest sort of balderdash, but I'd had more truth than I could process for one day. So I left it at that.

"Call New York," Lucius said, "and schedule the Xantex closing. Just like none of this happened. It's our only chance to clear this and get out in one piece."

"You mean *your* only chance."

"Just stay with me on this."

"I should just let you twist in the wind."

"We'll twist together. I promise you that."

It was as if my father were reaching out of whatever existential darkness he was cloaked in to slap me in the back of the head. The way he used to. I went to my office and opened the program that tracked our accounts. Sure enough, the Xantex escrow account was now something over $10 million, just as it should have been at this point in the deal. Six million of that amount was money from the Xantex investors, but the missing $4 million had been covered by a transfer from the contingency accounts on other deals. Eventually the thing would unravel. I called Super Wiener in New York.

"Terrible about Marshall," he said.

"Yes."
"Did you have any idea he was depressed?"
"No."
"He seemed fine to me."
"He was fine."
"Evidently not."
"I don't know."
"I have a conference room for Thursday."
"Marshall's funeral is Wednesday."
"So Thursday's too soon?"
"Make it Friday."
"Friday it is."

i left the office and wandered. I drifted east and started crying around Sixth Street. By the time I sat down in Lincoln Park I was bawling in earnest. Regular park bench denizens looked at me curiously, this specimen in pinstripes and Ferragamos suffering a public hysterical breakdown. I was amazed myself. I couldn't remember the last time I cried like that. Marshall, Marshall, Marshall. My darling one. On the escalator at Dupont Circle. Talking with the proprietor at Roney Brothers. Bent over his coffee table with my panties in his mouth. The love of my life.

Trick-or-treaters had found him. Three kids. They thought it was a Halloween prank. The front door of his house was open, there was a plastic pumpkin with a candle in it, they thought the place was welcoming business. They knocked, rang the bell, then poked their heads in and spotted the body in the living room.

He hadn't known, I decided. He hadn't known about my dad.

But he'd known plenty that he never shared with me.

"Come on, baby, it ain't that bad."

A young black dude, a pretty boy, on his way east.

"Oh, it is."

"Naw, it never is. Come with me. I cheer you up."

"I bet you would."

I brought it down to sniffles. He made faces at me until I finally laughed.

"Cheer you up good," he said again.

"Thank you. You already have."

"A'ight. You have a nice day."

That was not in the cards. As he walked away my eyes focused on a figure standing by a tree on the north boundary of the park. We stared at each other for maybe twenty seconds before I realized it was Drew. Drew fucking Gillespie. He was watching me cry. Why didn't he come over here and put his arms around me? All right, maybe I hadn't given him the nicest welcome to Washington. Okay, okay. I could make it up to him. Just as I decided what to do, I looked over and he was gone.

Just like a dumb movie.

Life's a boring enough movie, does it have to be dumb, too?

My boyfriend is dead; my old boyfriend is following me around.

"Drew!" I yelled.

No answer. I ran to the edge of the park.

"Drew!"

He was gone.

I trudged back up East Capitol to my apartment. What the fuck was this shit with Drew now? Seven messages on my answering machine. Five about Marshall. One from my mother in Cincinnati. And a hang-up.

"Crap."

I listened to the dial tone. Why was that so infernally irritating—that click of the breaking connection? I kicked off my shoes and fell on the bed. Very soon I was crying again. I jumped up and began pawing through all the junk in my place, looking for any memento of Marshall. I had the watch he'd given me, some clothes, an air letter from London, and a Christmas card. Oh yes, and my alpha-hydroxy skin cream. Was that it? My whip, but that was at his place. I didn't have a single photograph of us together. We hadn't documented our affair. We hadn't even admitted it in public.

The London letter he'd written in the spring; it was dated April 21. He missed me, he wished I were there, I would like this house in Holland Park. Then a joking reference to the English vice, our favorite little game.

Holland Park. Home of Arlie Ralston.

No mention of Ralston in the letter. A reference to a corner on Shaftesbury Avenue where, a month earlier, a raving street seer had told us to always stay together—"Never let her go," the loon had said, "or you'll always regret it." A romantic moment, thrilling and embarrassing all at once.

I needed to call my mother. But what to say. I'd never mentioned Marshall to her. The last guy I'd introduced her to was Jay Hixon's successor in New York, a banker at Bear Stearns named Wheatley. Ned Wheatley. The only gentile in his department. Not a Catholic, though. And Mother seemed less than thrilled with him. We met at Windows on the World, a good cornball thing to do. It turned out to be practically the last time I saw Wheatley. He transferred to Los Angeles, and anyway there was that German, the one who'd known Fassbinder and wanted to take pictures of me wearing exotic underwear. Mother didn't meet him.

I wondered what happened to those pictures. And then I thought: What if I died tonight? What would be lying around in my apartment that I wouldn't want shared? Nothing from Marshall, unfortunately. I riffled through my boxes of photographs, old postcards, the occasional printed e-mail. There was a cache of dirty letters from a married man I met in Baltimore, the summer after my first year of law school. I was much on his mind, the poor bastard. But he got his jollies, writing down what he would never do. Why did I still have the letters? Because they were the only love letters I'd gotten since college. People don't write anymore.

What else did I have?

A book Mother had given me, when I went off to Kenyon. Thomas à Kempis's *The Imitation of Christ*. I'd never read it. I thought of it as some kind of medieval self-help book, and anyway I was through with the church. Or so I thought as a college freshman. Now I opened it. Randomly.

> As long as we live in this world we cannot be fully without temptation, for, as Job says, the life of man upon earth is a warfare.

Sensible, if obvious, observation. I flipped around some more.

> Therefore, do not think yourself secure in this life, whether you are a religious or a lay person. Frequently, those who have been esteemed in the sight of people as most perfect have been allowed to fall the more grievously because of their presumption. Oh, how pure a conscience should he have who would despise all transitory joy and would never meddle with worldly business, and what peace and inward quiet should he have who would cut away from himself all busyness of mind, and think only on heavenly things.

I remember that Caroline was home from Mount Holyoke when Mother gave me this book. My sister was in high college-feminist dudgeon, frowning at poor Drew G. and cocooning on the back porch with *The Awakening* and *Ann Veronica*. She snapped out of it in medical school and married a doctor. Now I was the unmarried feminist. I was the one making my own way. "This can guide your life," Mother had said to me. "Remember: we're souls on a journey."

Souls on a journey.

Mother wouldn't believe my life. But maybe I wasn't giving her enough credit. Maybe nothing would surprise her. After all, she lived for thirty years with my father.

the next morning the phone rang at my desk at work. It was a lawyer I'd never heard of. He was calling about an envelope that had been entrusted to him with instructions to give it to me in the event of Marshall's death. His office was on Connecticut Avenue just south of Dupont Circle.

"I'm so sorry," he said to me, taking my hand.
"Did you know Marshall well?" I asked.

"I did some of his personal legal work over the last couple of years. I can't say I knew him well."

This lawyer must have been over fifty, but he combed his obviously dyed hair straight forward in a funny bang. Marshall trusted this guy?

"Did you do his will?"

"No. He had attorneys in Charlottesville, I understand, who handled that. No, I just did some small things for him, relating to his house purchase and so on. But about a month ago he came in and arranged for me to give you this envelope, in the event of his death."

"Strange."

"Yes. But not so strange, I suppose, if he had been thinking about killing himself."

"I don't believe he killed himself."

"Well, here is what he wanted you to have."

"Have you read it?"

"No, I haven't. I wasn't asked to read it."

"Marshall didn't say anything about what was in it?"

"Marshall was a reticent man."

"Yes, he was."

I looked at the envelope, at the fancy engraved return address.

"You say he brought you this about a month ago?"

"Early October."

"Did he seem upset?"

"No."

"Did this seem like an odd request to you?"

"Yes, it did."

Back at the office I opened the envelope. The letter was brief.

Darling,

If you are reading this, something has gone terribly awry, and we haven't had a conversation we should have had. Please go to my Calvert office, and there, in the back left of the walnut closet, you will find a strongbox. The combination is R44-L11-R38. Go in light and peace.

Love, Marshall

My phone was ringing, I had unanswered e-mail, the intercom was buzzing, but I stood up from my desk and walked out of the office. I waved the letter at the receptionist and stepped out on Second Street. I didn't know where I was going, but I didn't want to sit in that office and I didn't want to go back to Lincoln Park. Drifting south, I ended up at Duddington Place, in the shadow of the Southeast Freeway. I looked at the letter again. The Calvert Street office, it said. I looked around me at the cozy row houses. Was there a personal nightmare like mine hidden behind every one of those doors? If I just went up and knocked, would a stranger take me in and hide me?

I walked back home. I lay on my bed, trying to gather the resolve to go up to Calvert Street. The phone rang.

"Hello," I said.

"Hey," said Drew.

"Drew." My voice was toneless. He was on the other side of the universe.

"I'm sorry, Rosalind. I'm sorry I acted the way I did."

"It's okay."

"I saw you crying in the park."

"Why didn't you come over?"

"All I could think about was that Range Rover fucker."

"He's dead."

"What?"

"Marshall's dead."

"What? How?"

"He was shot."

"Rosie. Rosalind. I knew it. I knew something was fucked up here. I knew it when you first called me."

"Well, it's fucked up, all right."

"Who killed him?"

"They're saying he killed himself. I don't believe them."

"What do the cops say?"

"Just that. So far."

"I'm worried about you."

"I am, too."

"Let me come get you. Let me get you out of there."

"Not now. Not yet."

"When, then?"

"I need a few days."

"I'm coming over."

"No. No, don't. I won't be here."

"Where will you be?"

"At work."

"Not a good idea. What is this job of yours, anyway? First that guy who scammed with your dad and now this."

"I have a closing in two days. In two days, then it'll be over."

"I hope it's not over before that."

"Please, Drew. I'll call you. I promise."

"I don't know where I'll be."

"Just go home. Go back to Zanesville."

"That's what you want?"

I was quiet.

"If that's what you want," he said. "I'll call you from there."

"I'll call you next Monday, Drew. I promise. Thanks for checking on me."

"You're sure?"

"I'm sure."

He hung up. And I looked at the ceiling and felt a crushing, overwhelming weariness. My legs, I was sure, would never carry me up to Calvert Street. They did carry me to the refrigerator, where there was most of a quart of Breyers chocolate ice cream in the freezer. It wasn't long before it was gone.

on wednesday I was on my way to Charlottesville again, riding in another British vehicle. Lucius's Jaguar this time. Our destination was Marshall's funeral service. Various family members had handled the arrangements.

"He's old Charlottesville," Lucius said.

"Meaning what?"

"Meaning we'll feel out of place."

Up ahead, looming on the right, was the Roney Brothers

gun shop. My vision blurred, and though I tried to think of anything to stop crying—old Three Stooges routines, a loud fart I'd heard echoing in the ladies' room at the Uptown theater—the tears were mounting an assault on the lower rim of my eye, and it was a losing battle to keep them from spilling down my cheeks.

"I'm going to have to redo my makeup."

"You look good. You have that grieving widow thing going."

"Well, I am grieving."

"I'm sorry."

That was said neutrally, with no tilt toward either sincerity or irony, as far as I could detect. And I was listening, hard.

"Were you and Marshall friends?" I asked.

"We were business partners."

"So you weren't friends."

"Oh, we were. We had something in common. Southeast Asia."

"You mean the war?"

"Precisely. The war."

"You were in Canada."

"That was part of the war, babe. As much a part of the war as Vientiane. You didn't have to be at Khe Sanh to have been fighting that war."

I watched the road. My tears dried up.

"And I think," Lucius said, "that Marshall wasn't through with the war."

"He didn't like you, did he?"

"I wouldn't say that."

"What would you say?"

"I'd say he was ashamed of what he did in Laos. That he was looking for some way to atone. Make up for it."

"By laundering money?"

"I don't think so. That was a means to an end."
"What end?"
"I don't know. But I think he wanted to go back to Laos."
"Well, he'd mentioned that to me."
"Had he?"
"Nothing concrete. Just that it would be nice to visit there."
"I think he wanted to do more than visit. I think he was planning to live in exile there."
"In exile?"
"Like someone else I could think of."
I didn't rise to the bait.
"Have you ever," Lucius asked me, "met Arlie Ralston?"
"No."
"You should."
"Is he coming to the funeral?"
"Sent his regrets."
I kept watching the road.
"He's coming to New York. I want you to take him something for me."
"As part of my official duties as counsel to Rigel Associates?"
"Absolutely."
In the distance I could see the Blue Ridge Mountains. Could I flee into those hills, shed my clothes, live in the high pines like a wild woman, eating nuts and berries, on the run from this world? Disappear, like my father?
I looked at Lucius. He'd brought up Dad's name, at our first interview.
Is Dr. Robert Wilcox your father?
But not his real name. Not the whole man. Not the Ruslan Vilkos who left Pittsburgh when he was seventeen and

hitchhiked or walked or rode a freight to Wheeling, West Virginia. Who'd already worked digging coal after school and summers in a steel mill. Who got a job in an ice plant and then drove an ice truck door-to-door to make deliveries for the last people to have old-fashioned iceboxes. Who went part-time to West Liberty State College, who held his own with the older G.I. Bill students back from Europe or the Pacific, who charmed some kind of committee into giving him a few scholarship dollars. Who slid farther west, changed his name from Ruslan to Robert, and finished school at Ohio State in Columbus (Come Blow Us, I used to call it). Who after three years of hustling and four years of medical school met, beguiled, and married my mother, and she brought the young man now called Wilcox home to Zanesville and prevailed on her parents to help finance their modest first house. Who sired five daughters, including me. Who could, for all I knew, be wandering those distant Blue Ridge Mountains, hunkering down to await the future.

But I doubted it.

I wondered how much of that story Lucius knew.

The authorities hadn't found my father in more than five years of searching. There were theories: Canada, Mexico, even that he'd gone to the ancestral homelands in the indeterminate tangle of hills once known as Ruthenia. My own fantasy was that he was in Laos or Thailand. Probably Marshall-inspired, that one. But I could see Dad in Bangkok, master of an underground medical service ministering to the whores. Or maybe he ran drugs out of Burma. That was more his line. That was one of his many sidelines in Zanesville, as we found out after his arrest. Selling prescription drugs. Especially morphine.

I looked at Lucius. What if Dad was still his partner, his

secret partner, and they were still running a scam? This time on everybody. Two million each, at the end of the game.

"I quit," I said.

He watched the road. He pursed his lips, never looking my way.

"Did you hear me?"

"What was that?"

"I said I quit."

"Quit what?"

"This job."

He puffed his cheeks and pursed his lips, as if he were going to spit a gob of tobacco juice.

"It's a free country."

He kept watching the road.

We were waiting each other out, and we didn't say another word all the way to Charlottesville.

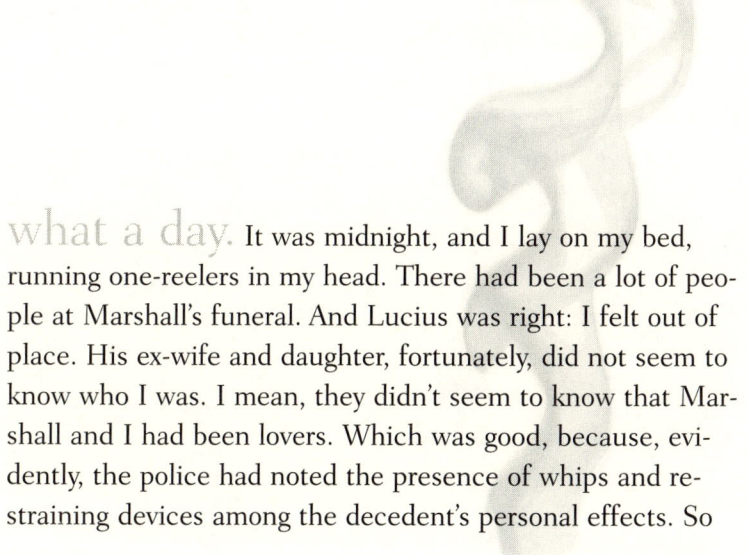

what a day. It was midnight, and I lay on my bed, running one-reelers in my head. There had been a lot of people at Marshall's funeral. And Lucius was right: I felt out of place. His ex-wife and daughter, fortunately, did not seem to know who I was. I mean, they didn't seem to know that Marshall and I had been lovers. Which was good, because, evidently, the police had noted the presence of whips and restraining devices among the decedent's personal effects. So

I was relieved on that score. Even though the wife was very perfunctory, almost dismissive, in dealing with me. She was a handsome woman, as I expected she would be. She didn't seem particularly grief-stricken. The eulogists were all strangers to me and were all drawn from Marshall's pre-Rigel life—the navy and the Agency and Wharton. I talked to the daughter, Priscilla, who looked just like her father, and we actually hit it off. We could relate. She hadn't thought her father was depressed, she said. I didn't either, I said. She was finishing up law school at Yale. We talked about the business of lawyering. "Save yourself," I said. "It's not too late." She laughed—quietly, so her mother wouldn't see—and said she'd always wanted to work in a bakery. Do it, I said. I could play undergraduate at Brown. Hell, I could play junior high school. In no time at all we were talking about men, rating the ones standing around the grave site. Of course I got handed a couple of cards. It's the human condition.

But one of the men at the funeral, one who received a very low rating from both me and Priscilla, was Gregory Payson. The FBI man. What, don't those guys ever turn it off? I couldn't believe he was standing there, at the back of the crowd at the cemetery. And I swear he winked at me.

"Hi, Greg," I said. "What are you doing here?"

"Paying respects."

"Were you Marshall's friend?"

"I think that could have happened."

"You're snooping, is what you're doing."

"Can we talk a minute?"

"About what?"

"May I call you Rosalind?"

"I suppose. Thank you for asking."

"You go by Roz?"

"I do not."

"Rosalind, then. Let's take a little walk."

So we did. Around the very pretty cemetery, winding among the gravestones. Lucius, of course, observed our departure. Later I lied to him about it. I didn't tell him what Payson told me, which went something like this:

"I'm assuming you know what I'm talking about when I tell you that Roos Van Zyk has appropriated a good sum of money from one of your firm's escrow accounts."

I was silent.

"You do know what I'm talking about?"

"I know there was a question about the escrow account. It's been resolved."

"He took it. Van Zyk. That's his prerogative. I guess you didn't know that. But it turns out to have been part of an agreement he made with Trevor Langford."

"I don't know anything about that."

"I know. I'm filling you in. You know why Van Zyk acceded to your terrorist provisions?"

"What? How do you know—"

"Because his ass is covered. It's a private business arrangement. He's got private protection. The government of South Africa is irrelevant. It doesn't matter if the current administration stays in power or if, as he said on a wiretap, 'a bunch of pod replicants from Andromeda take over.' His arrangements will be intact."

I became aware of my open mouth and made an effort to close it.

"Wait a minute," I said.

"Have you heard of Executive Resources?"

"We've had dealings with them. That's all I know."

"Do you know what they do?"

"Some kind of private security firm, I believe."

"Marshall was helping me with this. Now I need someone to take his place."

"Don't look at me."

"I'm looking at you."

"Hey, you had something on Marshall. You don't have anything on me."

"I'm appealing to your loyalty to Marshall."

"He's dead. We're attending his funeral."

"He was very loyal to you. He's why I don't have anything on you."

"What are you talking about?"

"You are the general counsel of Rigel Associates."

"Was. I just quit."

"In that capacity you facilitated illegal activity."

"I had no knowledge."

"I happen to believe you. Because of what Marshall told me."

"Well, as I said, I quit."

"What exactly does that mean? Were you fired?"

"No, I voluntarily relinquished the position."

"Effective when?"

"Effective immediately. Effective as soon as I told Lucius Atkinson. Which was on the drive down here."

"I think you should reconsider that decision."

"I won't."

"Marshall would want you to help me."

"How do you know that?"

"I just know it."

"What do you want me to do?"

"I want you to see the Xantex deal through. It would help our investigation if we had someone on the inside."

"Investigation of what?"

"Money laundering."

"Money laundering."

"And other things."

"What other things?"

"I'll tell you tomorrow. Will you come see me?"

I said I would. And so I had an appointment the next day, Thursday. Down at the Washington field office at Buzzard Point. The cloaca of the universe. To talk about money laundering. And other things.

"I wouldn't share this with Mr. Atkinson. For obvious reasons."

"He sees us talking. He's looking at us right now. What am I going to tell him?"

"Anything you want, except that we have an appointment tomorrow."

"Aren't you talking to him, too?"

"Eventually."

"I'll tell him you want to talk to me but we haven't arranged a time yet."

"I'm not telling you to lie."

"Of course you are." I gave him one of my better looks. One of the naughty ones. "But I don't need your permission to lie to men."

So I lied to Lucius on the drive home. I don't know if he believed me. I didn't really care. Since I had so melodramatically resigned my position, I briefly held the upper hand. Then he played his trump card.

"I'm not going to tell our Latter-Day Saint of a G-man about your father. Not yet, anyway."

My father. I thought about the card Drew gave me, the one with the Swiss bank account number on it. The one my dad hadn't given me himself. I could be killed for that number, I realized.

"Absalom, Absalom," I said.

Now I sat up at the edge of my bed. The book was right across the room. I walked over and took the raggedy paperback down from its brick-and-board shelf. But I put it back after a few pages. I can't read anything anymore.

I looked at my old LPs. Relics of another decade. Some dated from high school. Freshman year, Zanesville, 1981. I flipped through them. The Ramones. The Talking Heads. The Pretenders. And the years after, the years of first cars and first sex: Bryan Ferry, the Go-Go's, the Waitresses. Coming out of a car tape deck on a starlit highway shoulder. The Clash, *London Calling*. I wanted to go back. I wanted to go home. I wanted to be in the scarred moonscape of a strip mine with Drew Gillespie, far away from all this. I wanted to be in my father's arms.

I looked at the envelope containing the letter from Marshall and the combination to the strongbox. I needed to get to Calvert Street and look at that. There just wasn't time in the next couple of days.

Trevor Langford, Payson had said. Trevor Langford authorized Van Zyk to take the money. And I'd never even heard of him before last Friday afternoon. But Payson didn't mention my father. Maybe he didn't know. Or maybe Lucius made it all up.

Finally I fell asleep to the last track on *Remain in Light*: "The Overload," a song I had not heard in fifteen years. Long droning tones, the somnolent tapping snare, a vision of the desert, high-tension towers marching to the horizon, a cave surrounding me, engulfing me, slowly, like a black amoeba enfolding its prey.

at the Green Beard, having lunch with Claudia, I ordered the smallest house salad.

"I'm not hungry," I said.
"I'm not, either."
"I haven't eaten since it happened."
"Neither have I."

Mr. O'Shaughnessy flailed around in our general vicinity.
"God *damn* it, ladies! Slammed again!"

That greeted us as he brought our iced tea.

"They're backed up in the kitchen. Then they got the fucking orders mixed up." This was to tell us our food would be late. Then there was another harried pass: "I'm going down, girls. Follow the bubbles." Claudia and I looked at each other. In spite of ourselves, we were cheering up a little. Our man was serving only three tables.

"They've got me running fifteen different directions. I told Jimmy, why don't you just shove a broom up my ass and let me do the floor while I'm at it?"

"Ask for a raise," Claudia said.

O'Shaughnessy leaned in close. "From Jimmy? The lad's tighter than a baby's anus."

When our salads finally arrived, I told Claudia a little about my contact with the FBI. That I was going straight to an appointment with Greg Payson. That I didn't know what I should do.

"He wants me to cooperate with him."

"You mean, sell out Atkinson?"

"I'm not sure yet."

"You think Lucius is in trouble?"

"I don't know. We may all be in trouble."

"I knew something stank. I knew something was wrong."

"You were right."

"It's that deal we were working on the other night, isn't it?"

"It's part of it, evidently."

"Oh, God."

"You should find another job."

"I can't leave you now. Not in the middle of this."

"I'll keep you posted."

"What does this guy want from you?"

"He wants me to stay on and ride out the Xantex deal. Which is funny, because that's the same thing Lucius asked me to do."

O'Shaughnessy came back and stood by our table with his hands on his hips, glowering. Frayed shirt collar, tie as old as I was, filthy apron.

"Well, are you gals eating or what?"

"New diet, Mr. Shaugn."

"Life's too short to diet."

"That's what I used to think. Now I think it's too short not to."

the Washington field office of the FBI rented rooms in the ugliest building ever constructed, way down at the sour water confluence of the Anacostia and the Potomac, a place called Buzzard Point. I'd never been there before. It made the FBI headquarters, hideous as that was, look like a Beaux Arts masterpiece by Stanford White. I rode there in a taxi, and once we crossed K Street SW, we were in new territory for me.

"Nice ride down?" Payson asked me.

"What a shithole this is."

"I won't quarrel with that assessment."

"I guess you'd rather be in Salt Lake City."

"As a matter of fact I would."

"So what's up?"

"Why don't you tell me a little bit about your relationship with Marshall?"

"What do you want to know?"

"Did you know he kept guns at his house?"

"I knew that."

"That didn't strike you as odd?"

"I just went with it."

"He shot himself with a Sig Sauer .380."

I felt a little shudder behind my heart. I knew that gun.

"Shot himself."

"If he shot himself."

"Do you doubt it?"

"Yes, I do. What do you think?"

"I doubt it, too."

"Why?"

"It just didn't seem in character."

"Exactly."

"Can't you establish whether he killed himself? Isn't that your job?"

"He left no note." Payson looked at me. "And I think it's likely he would have communicated something to you. Suicides are always addressing someone."

"He wasn't addressing me."

"Do you know why I'm trusting you to help me?"

"No."

"I am trusting you."

"Okay."

"Had Marshall ever mentioned me to you?"

"No, he hadn't."

He leaned back in his chair and put his feet on the desk. It was an unexpected gesture. Not what I expected from a Mormon.

"There were no prints on the pistol except his," he said. "But there were a few odd things."

"What?"

"I'd rather not discuss them just yet."

I was thinking: should I tell him? I'd handled that gun. My prints should have been on it. It'd been wiped. If not by Marshall, then by the person who killed him.

"Please," I said. "Go ahead. Discuss them."

"Did you and Marshall like to play with handcuffs?"

"That's none of your business."

"I just want to ascertain that those items were basically innocuous."

"Actually, he preferred to be tied."

His eyes lit when I said that. I'd seen that light before. He shut it down quickly, but I'd glimpsed it. Oh, no. Why can't I stop myself? And a repressed Mormon, too. This could get out of hand quickly. I tried to change the subject.

"Tell me something," I said.

"What?"

"Explain something to me."

"If I can."

"What about these Brits?"

"What about them?"

"What's the story? I never heard of them—I swear—I never heard of them until last Friday afternoon. Marshall mentioned them, trying to fill me in on some things, I guess.

But he wasn't telling me the whole story. Or the real deal. How is it that in a year and a half of serving as general counsel to this outfit I never heard of the prime investors?"

"Because you weren't supposed to know about them. You were part of the front."

"Yeah, yeah, but how did all this get started? Do you know?"

"Not really. I'm confused about a couple of things. Mostly about Lucius Atkinson."

"Oh."

"But as far as Langford and Marshall, they met through Arlie Ralston."

"The Laos connection."

"The Bank of England has had MI5 watching Ralston for a long time. He has a long history as a money launderer. He'd just never been nailed."

"MI5?"

"The English FBI."

I looked at Payson and wondered if his English counterparts were any more impressive.

"Look," Payson said. "Trevor Langford and our friend Ralston set up Xantex as a money-laundering front back in 1981. We've determined that. Their South African partner is Roos Van Zyk. There's a security forces connection there. They all did consulting time at Executive Resources, back in the old South Africa, back in the eighties. At some point Langford told Ralston about this talented acolyte of theirs, Lucius Atkinson."

"The hippie draft dodger."

"He met Langford in Toronto. Langford recruited him."

I held my breath, waiting to hear the next chapter. The Zanesville chapter.

"They sent him to the London School of Economics, on Xantex's dime."

"Sent who?" I asked. That wasn't what I was expecting to hear.

"Atkinson. He did a year at the LSE, then they paired him up with Marshall. Rigel Associates was born. Marshall had been at First Boston. He'd developed an expertise in project finance. They decided to start running the Xantex money through Rigel, and into legitimate business ventures. They used Marshall's connections. That's why you were a project finance firm."

"We had straight clients, too. That's all I knew about."

"Yes, you did. That was the beauty of it."

He was leaving out my dad. Either he was playing with me, or he didn't know.

I thought about how Drew Gillespie had connected Lucius and my father by looking at court papers. But Lucius hadn't been a defendant in those trials. And they were state charges. But a federal indictment had been pending. And the FBI had nosed around. Had they just overlooked the connection? It was a big pile of papers, I'm sure. And caseloads are heavy.

"Why did Marshall leave First Boston and agree to do this?"

"Good question. I was hoping maybe you could give me some insights into that."

"I have no idea. Every day that passes I realize I know less about him."

"You were important to him."

"Then why didn't he tell me anything?"

"I think he was planning to."

"When?"

"Soon."

"Why did he come to you? Or were you onto him?"

"Things are unraveling at Rigel."

"No kidding."

"There's a fight going on."

"A fight."

"A battle for control. And the outside heat, I mean Scotland Yard and MI5, was turning up. Big-time. On the Brits, I'm talking about now. Outside directors, you might call them. Marshall wanted to cut Xantex loose as a client, try to take the firm straight."

"Is that what he told you?"

"Something like that."

"And then he turns up dead."

Payson nodded.

"Where was Van Zyk at the time of the murder?" I asked.

"Murder? It could be a suicide."

"Whatever. You told me Van Zyk moved the money in the escrow account. Did Marshall tell you that?"

"He did."

"Van Zyk doesn't seem very happy about it. In fact, I get the impression he doesn't know where the money is." I was thinking of Lucius and his obvious fear of Van Zyk. But of course Lucius could have been jerking me around.

"The last thing Marshall told me was that the money had been restored to the account. That whatever went on, there was a temporary borrowing. Just a movement between accounts."

Well, yes, I thought: there was the $10 million in there now. But Lucius had said the original $4 million was not part of that sum. I just nodded at Payson. It was all too complicated and ridiculous.

"So where was Van Zyk on Sunday?" I asked.

"Well, he was on a plane to Miami. And now he's on his way back."

"He is?"

"Don't you know? You have a closing tomorrow in New York."

"Oh. Right."

"I need a report from you on what happens there. I need to know the truth, when the time comes to move on these guys."

"The truth."

"Very occasionally it becomes relevant."

"so did he convert you?"

Lucius startled me so much I jumped.

"Jesus, you scared me. What are you talking about?"

"Our man Payson. Did he call up visions of Moroni?"

"When? What do you mean?"

"On your walk around the cemetery."

Oh, that. I was relieved he didn't know about my trip to Buzzard Point.

"He didn't mention it. I told you. He wanted me to come to FBI headquarters tomorrow. I said I was busy."

"Lubyanka West. You know all those starlings that shit on the building? Those are the ghosts of the souls J. Edgar tormented."

Claudia brought me the latest closing document drafts from Winslow.

"So we're on track?" Lucius peered at the cover pages.

"We're on."

"Good. Can you come in my office?"

Claudia gave me a look, then gathered the documents in her arms and hurried away.

Lucius ushered me into his office and closed the door.

"I have something for you," he said.

He handed me a thick manila envelope.

"I want you to give this to Arlie Ralston in New York."

"What is it?"

"It's a contract proposal."

"May I look at it?"

"Sure."

It was written in Cyrillic. None of it was comprehensible to me.

"Is this Russian?"

"Bulgarian. Similar."

"What's going on?"

"Possible project. Gas-fired power plant near Sofia. Cheap Caspian energy. It's just a possibility. But I want Arlie to get a jump on it."

Here was the casual deployment of that name again, a figure Marshall had described as being from the distant past. From the Vientiane of 1972. I was five in 1972. Finishing kindergarten and learning to ride a bicycle. It was all just background noise: Martin, Bobby, Nixon, Vietnam.

"Why have I never heard of Arlie?"

"You said you had heard of him."

"Yeah. Last Friday. You've obviously done business with him for years."

"Only peripherally."

"So we have Bulgarian clients? It's news to me."

"Don't you have enough to do?"

"I suppose I have enough to do."

"Plenty on your plate?"

"Watch it."

"We know you're just one person. We assigned you one segment of our business. The rest gets done in London."

"You didn't tell me it was a segment of your business. I thought it was all of your business."

"Just do this little chore for me."

"Why should I?"

"You're still drawing pay."

"I can afford to live without it."

"If you still want to quit, quit."

"If I still wanted to quit, I wouldn't be here."

"Good. I'm glad you're on board."

"On board what, is the question. Aren't you afraid of Van Zyk?"

"You can handle him."

"Why has Van Zyk been so interested in me?"

"The same reasons a lot of men are interested in you."

"I never saw him face-to-face this whole last year, the whole time we're doing this Xantex deal, and suddenly he shows up in Washington and he's all over me."

"He's all over a lot of women, sweetheart. Don't flatter yourself too much."

"He's after my father, isn't he?"

"He knows nothing about your father."

I had realized by now that I was not the lie detector I had fancied myself to be. I didn't know what I believed.

"You have any instructions for Winslow?" I asked.

"No. I know you'll handle this."

"All right."

"And when you see Roos?"

"Yes?"

"Don't mention Arlie."

"Don't they know each other?"

"Yes, they do."

"But you're holding out on somebody."

"Someday I'll explain."

"Those were my dad's last words to my mother."

"You seem to have some trust issues."

"Shouldn't I?"

we sat around a conference table on the Forty-seventh floor of the Triangle Trust Building: me, K.A., Super Wiener, my old bedmate Jay Hixon, Van Zyk, one of Van Zyk's South African partners, and two London solicitors I'd previously communicated with only by fax. Once again, I was the only woman in the room. K.A. ran the meeting. Everything was oiled. Jay Hixon wouldn't look at me. Neither would Super Wiener, except when I wasn't looking at him.

I'd look up and he'd look away. Not that I cared anymore. Now that I knew it was all a game.

Van Zyk, on the other hand, looked at me steadily. Stared, in fact. I had instructions to meet Arlie Ralston at a bench in Roosevelt Park, near the corner of Forsyth and Delancey. Lucius's melodramatic touch. I asked him why such a grubby location, and he said it had private significance. For him and Arlie. "Fill me in," I said, and he said, "I can't." That was that.

"Everyone seems happy," K.A. said. Then, looking at me: "Is everyone happy?"

"I'm happy," I lied.

"Very happy," said Van Zyk.

"Super," said K.A.

"Wonderful," said Super Wiener.

"Let's sign," Van Zyk said.

I'd made a Xerox of the Bulgarian documents Lucius gave me, and I'd sent them to Payson. So far nothing of any interest to the FBI had happened at this closing meeting. The parties signed the contracts, and we all shook hands. Some kind of paralegal or underling brought in a small bottle of champagne and poured a glass for everyone.

"To the future," K.A. said.

On our way out of the conference room I gave Hixon a friendly little elbow shove. He didn't respond. They were all treating me as if I didn't exist. I understood. Marshall was dead. He wasn't protecting me anymore.

Well, fuck them.

Only Van Zyk was being friendly. Going down in the elevator, he put his hand on the nape of my neck and slowly let it slide south along my spine. It was a nice move, executed with great confidence, and I thought about what Lucius and

Marshall had said about his womanizing. There's something about a skilled womanizer, after all. Part of me hates them, but another part of me harbors an abstract admiration of good technique. I was weighing a response, but before I came to any decision the doors opened on the lobby and there was suddenly two feet of airspace between us. We exited to the plaza through separate adjacent revolving doors, picking our way among the commissioned lumps of twisted metal that disfigure every public space south of Fulton Street; the money changers think they can buy a secular heaven with bad art. As we approached William Street the gap between us closed; as he hailed a cab with his left hand his right arm pulled me next to him; by the time the door on the old Checker closed I was meeting his jaded tongue with my own. We'd crawled up William Street to Beekman, headed to Park Row, before I regained control of myself. I was thinking of that Halloween mask and a Sig Sauer .380.

And my dream of Dirk Bogarde.

"Where do you want to go?" he asked me.

"How about this place Lucius likes? It's on Mercer Street."

"It must be a terrible place."

"Depends on your tastes."

"I mean, if Lucius likes it."

"Well, I like it, too."

"Let's go."

at the bar on Mercer Street we sat at the very table where Lucius had interviewed me for this job. I was perched on the very seat I'd occupied nearly a year and a half ago, when all this so innocently began. What had I done? I'd answered an ad. That was all. I'd answered an ad and accepted a job. That was it. Things could have been different. I could have poached a partner at Winslow by now. I could have been pregnant on Park Avenue.

But they'd wanted me to answer that ad. What would they have done if I'd passed on it, gone somewhere else?

"Do you miss Marshall?" Van Zyk asked me.

I looked at him, trying to decide what he knew.

"He was a good boss," I said. "I enjoyed working for him."

"Speaking frankly, I was getting very worried about him."

"How do you mean?"

"I wasn't surprised when he killed himself."

"When did you hear the news?" I asked.

"Monday morning. In Miami."

"Did you see him on Sunday?"

I couldn't decide if I was really looking at a killer. Van Zyk had been in Miami when Marshall died, Payson told me. But I knew Marshall didn't pull the trigger on that Sig.

"I didn't. But I know where he was."

"Where was he?"

"He was with you."

"How do you know that?"

"I just do."

I looked up at the ceiling, which was a huge fish-shaped skylight. I had just under an hour until my secret appointment with Arlie Ralston.

"Would you like something to eat?" Van Zyk asked.

"I'm not hungry."

"Another drink? A real one this time?" I was just drinking a tonic water.

"Not just yet, thank you."

"You were in such a good mood a little while ago."

"That was a little while ago."

"Such a friendly mood."

"Moods change."

He slammed back his whiskey and signaled for another one.

"Martinis are the specialty here," I said.
"Have one. Please. On me."
"Just another plain tonic, please."
"No gin?"
"No gin."

The slinky waitress brought the drinks, and Van Zyk reached across the table to take my hand. I pulled it away, placed it safely in my lap.

He looked at me with implacable blue eyes. Our eyes were the same color, I observed.

And yes, I'd sent him confusing signals. A tongue kiss can be fairly interpreted as an invitation to further intimacy. But that was my prerogative, to be confusing. And I'd decided that he was in fact a killer.

"A woman is a minefield," he said, "disguised as the Garden of Eden."

Well, what about men? They don't even bother with the disguise.

"Sorry," I said. "I guess I was bored. Every time I sit through a closing I want to kiss somebody."

"And I was the Johnny-on-the-spot."

I took out a cigarette. Would he light it, or had he given up the game?

He lit it.

"I realize," he said, "that you've been left in the dark about certain aspects of this transaction. I regret that. But it was for convenience. And for your own protection. Don't be angry."

"I'm not exactly angry."

"I want you to meet somebody."

"I've heard that before."

He took out a cell phone, and for a moment I was afraid he was somehow in league with Arlie Ralston, that they were going to shove my face into Lucius's duplicity, and who knew what after that.

"Trevor. Roos."

But no. He was speaking to Trevor Langford. The secret director, according to Greg Payson.

"We're at the pub. Right. Eighty-nine Mercer Street. You'll see us at the back of the room. Righto."

He put his phone back in his jacket pocket and raised his drink.

"I'm glad we're having this little chat," he said.

"What chat?"

"The one we'll be having when Trevor arrives."

"I've never met Mr. Langford."

"It'll be a treat."

"Are you going to tell me what's going on?"

"Yes."

I hadn't expected an answer that simple. I hadn't expected an answer at all. But then again, I should have relied on past experience. No man has ever sat across from me for very long and kept his mouth shut.

"What's going on is this," he said. "There are going to be some management changes at the firm."

"Which firm? Xantex?"

"Rigel Associates."

"Oh."

"I'll explain them when Trevor arrives."

"He's part of the new order, I gather."

"Oh, he was part of the old order. You just didn't have the whole picture."

"But I've learned a lot, this last week or so."

Van Zyk looked into my eyes, and I could feel it coming. Another lecture.

"There are two kinds of people in this world," he said. "The governors and the governed. It's always been that way."

"Always."

"And it always will be. It's just a question of who wields the lash."

"I've had experience in that line." Shut the fuck up, I told myself.

"As have I."

"And you want to keep doing it."

"I want to keep the reins in the right hands."

"In the white boys' hands."

He turned to look at the front of the room. Someone was coming in. I turned to see a tall thin man in a long fur-trimmed tweed overcoat. He was wearing leather gloves, which seemed excessive given the relatively mild weather.

"How did you get here so fast?" I blurted, without being introduced.

"I was in the neighborhood." Plummy accent. "You must be Miss Wilcox."

"Rosalind."

"How do you do? I'm Trevor Langford."

"I know."

"She knows," said Van Zyk.

"Well, Rosalind, we have a mutual friend."

"Had."

"Yes. Just so. Had. Very sad, that."

"Very."

"I understand you were with him the day he died."

"Where were you?"

Langford sat down next to Van Zyk. He pulled off his gloves. They looked at each other. Then they looked back at me.

"Hey, understand this," Trevor said. "You report to us. We don't report to you."

I stood up. I recognized his voice, and the accent, and the "hey." My ears were tingling, and I wondered if I'd turned visibly red. He was the one on the phone. The one hanging up on me. Fuck me to tears.

"Understand this," I said. "I don't do anything if I don't feel like it."

"Wait. Please. I'm sorry." Langford was beside me in an instant. He held the back of my chair for me, like a gentleman. He signaled for the waitress. "Please sit down."

It seemed like a very long run to the door. Something told me to flee out into the falling darkness, run to Penn Station, and forget my rendezvous with Arlie Ralston. Pack my things and take a bus to the heartland. Say good-bye to Rigel Associates. Now and forever. Something told me all that.

"All right," I said. I sat down. So often I've ignored good advice, even when it comes from myself.

"Martinis are the specialty here," Roos said to Trevor.

"Is that right? Is that what you recommend, Rosalind?"

"Suit yourself."

"Oh, be nice. I'm the client, remember."

"That's not what I'm hearing."

Van Zyk whispered in Langford's ear. Then he turned to me.

"Yes, well, what we're here to tell you officially, Rosalind, is that Trevor is a principal in Rigel Associates."

"He's not on the incorporation agreement."

"Not the one you've seen."

"Then he's a silent partner. A secret illegal interest."

"Well, now, that's a matter of interpretation. We have legal opinion that says we're not breaking the law."

"What did that cost?"

"Quite a bit."

"Worth it, I hope."

"Hasn't been tested yet. But now that Marshall is no longer with us, Trevor is going to be assuming the role of head of the firm."

"And why am I hearing this from you instead of from Lucius, the current partner of record?"

"Lucius. Yes. Well, I think his future role is going to diminish."

"Diminish."

"Yes. I think so."

"Why should what you think matter?"

"Because I am Rigel Associates' biggest client. Without Xantex, there's nothing."

"Not true. We're part of dozens of deals."

"But all the capital comes from Xantex. That's why Trevor is coming on board."

Trevor was served his martini. He looked at his watch, crooking his wrist to slide back his shirt cuff.

"I don't have much time," he said. "Unfortunately I must be off soon."

"Me, too," I said.

"Where do you need to be?" asked Van Zyk.

"Never mind."

"Oh, not another date."

"My business."

"Indeed."

They looked at each other again.

"Well," Trevor said. "Let me be brief. We'd like you to be part of the new regime. We'd like you to stay on as part of our counsel staff."

"Part."

"It's a fact that most of the legal work for Xantex is done in London. But we may keep the Washington office open. Part of that decision depends on whether you'll consent to stay."

"You promised to tell me what's going on."

"What's going on is business as usual," Van Zyk said. "That's what we want you to understand. And we want you to understand something else, about the nature of the contracts you'll be drafting."

"May or may not be drafting," I said.

They looked at each other again.

"I'm on the board of another organization," Trevor said. "You may have heard of it. An outfit called Executive Resources."

"I've heard of it. I've seen the name on some of our contracts. Security services, is it? Rent-a-cops?"

"More than that. We provide military services and consulting. Hardware and manpower."

"Mercenaries?"

"Professional soldiers, I prefer to call them. Veterans of the South African army, most of them. A few Sandhurst and St.-Cyr graduates as well. Quality personnel."

"St.-Cyr? Sounds like a Catholic girls' school."

"It's the French military academy."

"I see."

"Xantex has hired Executive Resources to guarantee the

integrity of our power lines to the diamond mine. De Beers, of course, has an interest. My point is, terrorism is not a major concern for us."

"And what does this have to do with me?"

"You always had quite a bee in your bonnet about force majeure provisos in Xantex contracts. And we really don't want all the fuss. We'd just as soon not have attention drawn to the subject. Seeing as how we've taken care of matters. You get my point?"

"Hey, don't confuse me with someone who gives a shit. I'm happy to sit and draw pay. Now that I get your point."

"It's just that we don't want to jeopardize our standing with the big investment houses. You understand."

"You like getting calls from Morgan Stanley."

"We want them to take our money, that's all."

"Oh, I don't think they're all that particular. Not from what I've seen."

Langford killed his drink and pulled on his gloves.

"Well, it was delightful meeting you, Rosalind. I really must be going. I hope you'll consider staying on with us. I'll be seeing more of you soon. I hope."

"Good-bye."

"Good-bye."

When he was gone, I told Van Zyk that I had to be going, too.

"Oh, sit with me a minute."

"No, Roos, I really have to go. I'm late."

"For what?"

"All right. Just for a minute."

He lit another cigarette for me.

"Are you planning to get married, Rosalind? Have children?"

"Who are you, my mother?"

"I'm just curious."

"I don't know. I have no idea. I take it one day at a time."

"I'm looking to get my children out of South Africa."

"Why?"

"I don't think they have a future there."

"You said Africa would boom. Someday."

"That's very long-run."

"The one where we're all dead."

"Precisely."

"Well, don't bring them here."

"Why not?"

"It's tough for kids here, too. You should see my sister, fretting over what preschool the kids will get into. And I want to laugh at her, but I know why she's worried. There's no middle ground anymore. It's Yale or jail."

"I can get them settled in England. I'm working it out."

"Roos, I've got to go. Really."

"Stay."

"No, really. I'm leaving. Thank you for the drinks."

He signaled for the check and reached across the table to keep me from getting up.

"Just one more thing, Rosalind."

"What?"

"I need to ask you something."

"What?"

"About your father."

I stubbed out my cigarette and stood up. "Shit," I said. "That lying fucking bastard."

"Your father?"

"Lucius Atkinson."

"Yes, indeed."

"Good-bye, Roos."

"I need to speak to your father."

I started walking toward the door. Van Zyk threw some money on the table and followed me. Outside on the street, he pressed me against the wall. I hadn't been in that position in years—involuntarily backed against a wall.

"Roos."

He was squeezing my wrists, hard, and trying to kiss me on the mouth. I was disgusted with myself for being aroused. But I was also angry enough to override my hormonal imperatives.

"Roos, let go. You're hurting me."

He relaxed his grip, just slightly, and kissed me on the forehead.

"I mean it, Roos. I'm going to scream. Right here."

It was not a deserted street. People were all around.

"You're not going to scream."

He opened his arms and stepped away from me.

"Let's go somewhere," he said.

"I am. I'm late for an appointment, and I'm going. Good-bye."

"Where we can be alone."

"No."

"Do you know why you were hired for this job?"

"I have some theories."

"We thought your father might try to contact you."

"Who is we?"

"All of us who wanted him to pay us what he owed us. You see, your man Lucius got his equity stake in Rigel Associates from the profits on your father's piddling little operations."

"If they were so piddling, why do you care?"

"Because when he disappeared, he took two million dollars of that pooftah Atkinson's equity stake. And that was our personal money. We had to make it up out of our own pockets, not with our investors' money. You see? I didn't find out for a long time. I didn't find out until the beginning of 1998. Then I gave the pooftah a year to get the money back. That's where you came in."

"I have no idea where my father is."

"Marshall didn't want us to hire you. I've always wondered why."

"Good-bye, Roos."

"Especially since he ended up fucking you."

"I said good-bye." I started walking away, south to Broome, and then left. Van Zyk followed me. At first he stayed a few steps behind. Then he speeded up, closing the gap between us.

"Leave me alone," I said.

He didn't answer. I started to run. East on Kenmare, across Mott and Elizabeth, headed to Roosevelt Park and the corner of Forsyth and Delancey. I was still two blocks away when I saw the police lights. Two cruisers pulled up on Chrystie and Forsyth, one pointed south, one pointed north. There was a man slumped on a park bench, with a bloody hole in his head. I knew before I saw his jacket that it was Arlie Ralston. The jacket was to be the identifier for our meeting. A hunting garment. Very British. I stopped running. The cops looked at me curiously.

"Did you hear anything, lady?" one said.

"No."

Van Zyk was a block away from me, standing still. As I watched he stepped away and disappeared up the Bowery.

"Why were you running?"

"I'm lost."

"Where you need to get to?"

"Chinatown."

"You gotta go south from here. Catch a taxi on the Bowery. You'll be there in two minutes."

"Thank you."

I pulled out my cell phone and tried to dial Lucius. The battery was dead.

"Fuck!"

I threw it against the concrete curb. It broke open, the parts scattering.

"Piece of shit!"

I kicked the plastic carcass and ran south on Chrystie, along the dark park, afraid to move back west, afraid of Van Zyk. Afraid of hidden doorways, of trash-strewn basements. Afraid my last sight might be a filthy brick wall. Another one-reeler: on my knees with Trevor Langford's gun at my head, him pulling the trigger the way he must have pulled it on Arlie Ralston, without even the pretense of a civil English greeting.

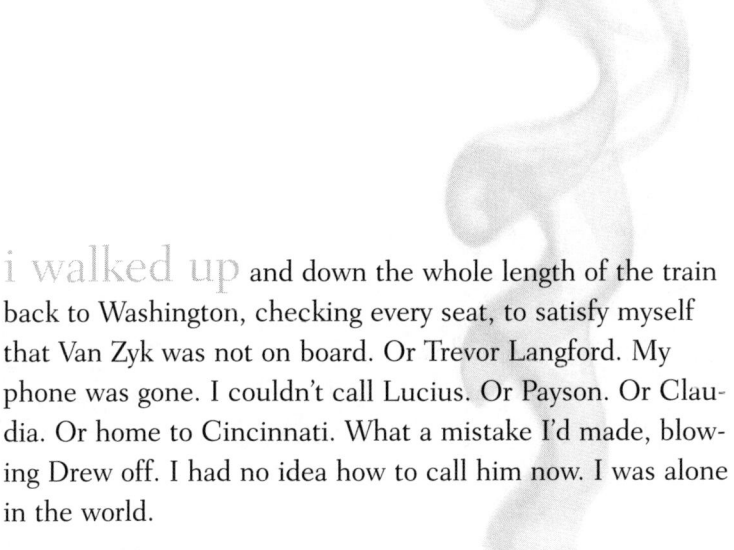

i walked up and down the whole length of the train back to Washington, checking every seat, to satisfy myself that Van Zyk was not on board. Or Trevor Langford. My phone was gone. I couldn't call Lucius. Or Payson. Or Claudia. Or home to Cincinnati. What a mistake I'd made, blowing Drew off. I had no idea how to call him now. I was alone in the world.

It was one in the morning when I arrived at Union Station. A taxi took me home to East Capitol Street. Standing on the stoop of my building, I had that feeling of being watched again. Opening the front door, trying to work the key, I was sure that the deathblow was coming down on my neck any second. I could sense it. I could feel it coming down, the blade millimeters from my hair, microseconds from slicing through to my skin and down to the bone, through the spinal cord, through the carotid arteries, it was coming *now*.

I whirled around but no one was there.

Upstairs in my apartment I locked the door and looked at the blinking answering machine, the digital 2 of the message enumerator glowing red in the darkness. I didn't want to play the messages.

I lay down in the dark. I didn't think I could possibly go to sleep, but I did.

I had a dream. I was in a dark, spongy landscape, something like lichen, purplish, horizon to horizon, and I was bouncing slowly up into the air, hundreds of feet at a time. I could just will myself into the air, rising up and then drifting laterally, losing altitude as I lost will, but able to sustain myself aloft by concentrating. I would let myself touch down long enough to spring back up, I'd flex my legs and jump, pushing away from the mossy ground, and I would drift back up in ecstatic suspension, crossing the countryside in huge arcs, parabolic launches into the cool dark sky. And there was something else in this dream. Another person. A naked figure, beckoning to me, drawing me toward him, pulling me down from my slow high glide over the lichen landscape and into a different scene. Rougher ground, the scarred land around a strip mine. Silhouetted behind him was the baroque and ornate wreck of a fantastically proportioned digging machine, a massive filigree of broken cables and rusted crane arms and giant sprocket wheels. The figure reached out, standing thigh-deep in a stream fouled by tailings. I heard his voice, speaking to me. Guiding me.

I woke up.

"Drew?" I said aloud, to the empty room.

in the morning I walked to work through a completely changed landscape. Every previously innocuous bush on North Capitol, every drowsily reassuring row house facade on Second, now radiated potential menace. I was looking at the parallel negative of the world I'd casually taken for granted before. A world lost to me now. I opened the door at Rigel Associates expecting to be cut down by a machine-gun fusillade. Claudia was in her office, wide-eyed, staring at the wall.

"Claudia," I said, "go home. Don't come back."

"Lucius wants to see you."

"Did you hear me? It's not safe here."

"I heard you. Lucius is waiting."

"Go home."

From across the hall I heard Lucius's voice.

"Rosalind! Get in here!"

I took my time. Lucius looked like he hadn't slept since I left for New York. And, looking again, I realized he hadn't. He was in the same clothes. And I almost thought I could smell him. Maybe I was imagining that.

"What the fuck are you doing?" he shrieked.

"I beg your pardon."

"You're talking to the FBI."

"You've been lying to me, Lucius. I don't feel any particular personal loyalty to you."

"Now I'm going to have to talk to them, too. I want to know what you've said."

"You better just tell the truth. We both better. If Trevor Langford doesn't kill us all first. You know Arlie Ralston is dead."

"I know."

"You know Langford killed him."

Lucius looked at me, then made a peculiar grimace I'd never seen on him before. He pounded on his forehead with the heels of his hands.

"You know Langford is taking over the firm. That your days are numbered. In this job, anyway, if not on this earth."

"We can't panic. We can't panic."

"Van Zyk knows about my dad. You lied your ass off. I'm going to Payson, and I'm just going to tell him how it is."

"You'll be implicated."

"I'm not worried about the FBI. It's what you said. We're in danger from Van Zyk. And Langford. You're right about something else: Marshall was talking to the feds. That's why he's dead. And we're next."

"One more day. I need one more day."

"To get out of town?"

"To get this money thing straight."

"If my father has it, I can't help you."

"I mean to get this deal passed off to another underwriter."

"The deal is closed. That's done. That has nothing to do with the trouble we're in."

"We just need to hide this mess long enough to get somebody to take it off our hands. We'll call it a restructuring and pay them a couple of points. And Rigel can peacefully go out of business."

"Oh, you're dreaming. You're back at the sundial on College Walk, and it's the Age of Aquarius."

"Don't play worldly with me. You were so easy to snow. You were like General Counsel Barbie. Baby's first job."

That was it. I smashed him over the head with a four-inch-thick SEC filing I snatched up off his desk. His aviator glasses went flying. Then I kicked over his computer monitor and stormed out, an ex–general counsel, wondering if I'd collect my last paycheck without hassle or if there'd be some kind of arbitration proceeding. That actually went through my mind.

"you can be such a bitch, Rosalind."

There I was, hearing it again. This time from Valerie Bernstein, Half-Smoke's new girlfriend. Thanks to me. You'd think there'd be some gratitude.

"I'm sorry if I'm not in a good mood."

We were having a quick lunch at the Brasserie. The joint where Ted Kennedy notoriously had it off with a lobbyist right on the floor of the upstairs dining room, between dessert and the check. Valerie wanted to tell me how well things were going. Girl stuff.

Today I wasn't eating.

"Things haven't been going well," I said.

"I know," she said, but of course she didn't know. She had no idea. "That's so terrible, that partner killing himself."

"It was terrible."

"You look tired. And you're losing weight."

"I haven't eaten in days."

"That's not good, Rosalind."

I kept looking around. I made sure we were seated so I could watch the door. Valerie told me about the dates she'd been on with Half-Smoke, how sweet he could be when he was drunk, how they'd both gone to the same camp in upstate New York just two years apart and they remembered the same dopey counselor who was famous for having had BenGay put in his jockstrap; he ran screaming off the tennis court and was forever known as "Great Balls of Fire."

Now I knew how war veterans felt. They came back from watching their comrades' heads explode to listen to Wal-Mart ads or their wives talk about the mean woman at work who keeps track of every minute they're in the bathroom and dumps food from the office refrigerator on an arbitrary and capricious basis.

Down that road lay madness, I knew. So I smiled at Valerie and said, "I'm happy for you," and drank another iced tea. I smoked a cigarette, too, trying to hold on to the small things. It seemed like the wise thing to do.

at Payson's wretched Buzzard Point office, I told him the story.

"You're sure it was Langford," he said.

"Of course I am. Do you want to hear it again?"

"No. And thank you. This is very helpful."

"Have you figured out that Bulgarian stuff I gave you?"

"I'm having it translated. I can't really discuss it, anyway."

"Oh, so you're going to fuck me over, too."

"That material could be very sensitive. Please bear with me."

"A gas-fired power plant in Sofia is sensitive?"

"Beg pardon?"

"Lucius told me the papers concerned a power plant."

"Not unless that plant produces counterfeit CDs."

"Then tell me something, at least. Make me feel better. I'm very nervous about those two."

"Langford?"

"And Van Zyk. They're killers."

"Well, I think the Bulgarian business was an attempt by Atkinson to make a connection outside of Xantex."

"So Ralston is dead."

"Murdered."

"Like Marshall."

"Well, we know someone killed Marshall."

"You confirmed that?"

"The bullet in his head didn't match the gun he was holding. Someone fired that gun, holding it in Marshall's hand, after he was already dead."

"Van Zyk."

"Well, he was in Miami. We know that for sure."

"Langford."

"Very possibly."

"He's killing witnesses."

"They were fighting over money. They were fighting over access to the capital conduits feeding Xantex. Atkinson and Ralston were in an alliance, trying to fend off a takeover by Langford and Van Zyk."

"I think they know I'm talking to you."

"How could they know that?"

"They knew Marshall was talking to you. That's why they killed him. Now they're killing everybody else."

"If you're really afraid, maybe you should go to a hotel. I might be able to arrange to pay for it, if you give me a couple of days."

"That could be a rough couple of days."

"We're looking for them. Hard. We could catch them any minute."

"Or not."

"Actually, I think they're still in New York. I have reason to believe that."

"I have a bad feeling they're not."

"Where do you think they are?"

"Here."

"In D.C.?"

"They're after me. They know I know Langford killed Ralston."

"You're not an official witness in this investigation."

"I'm not?"

"No. And believe me, you don't want to be. So it's up to you what you do. If you think you should hide out, hide out."

"What do you think?"

"I can't advise you."

"What, are you afraid of being sued?"

"You're the lawyer."

"Maybe Moroni will protect me."

"You never know."

i walked Claudia down A Street toward Lincoln Park. Leaves swirled in little tornado eddies on the sidewalk.
"Lucius wants me at my desk," she said.
"Fuck Lucius."
"Rosalind."
"Listen, you've got to stay out of the office. Just stay home."
"Lucius says you're crazy. You've lost your mind, he says."

"Do you believe him?"

"No."

"Then do what I say. Don't show up until I tell you it's safe."

"Well, I did what you asked. I told the cleaning crew not to come back this week."

"Did they understand you?"

"Yes. Eventually. And the receptionist quit."

"Back to Australia?"

"Moving to New York. Engaged to be married."

"Well, woo-woo."

"I wish I were getting married."

"Don't worry. It'll happen. And way too soon."

"I don't know, Rosalind."

"Know what?"

"This is all so weird."

We sat down in the park. On the same bench from which I'd last spied Drew. I looked at the tree he'd been standing beside, almost believing he would still be there.

"The day we heard about Marshall, I was sitting on this bench and I saw a guy I knew in high school standing over by that tree."

"What?"

I said it again.

"That's weird."

I had a vision then. As the cliché goes, my whole life passed before my eyes. And I wasn't even dying, as far as I could ascertain. Maybe I was being born again. But my mind flashed picture after picture, trying to account for my presence on this bench in Lincoln Park at this moment, this culmination of a string of events. I wanted there to be some kind of connection, some kind of order. I was three years old, pouring salt down my throat, thinking it was sugar, and vomiting in a wastebasket. I was in the back room of our first house in Zanesville, watching my two-year-old sister walk around naked in the midst of toilet training, her bottom soiled. I was with the whole family at Mount Rushmore; Mother was hugely pregnant with the twins. I was nine years old, touring the hospital with my dad, one of the only times he ever gave me a solo glimpse of his work life. I was sitting in the junior high library, looking up from *To Kill a Mockingbird* to see seven boys looking back at me, some sweet, some pricks. It was my fourteenth birthday and I was in my bedroom in the big new house we'd moved into when I was eight, listening to my mother scream at my father, hearing the low rumble of his patient, tolerant dismissals spurring her to ever more impassioned shrieking. I was in the basement of the school doper's house, putting aside my geometry homework to practice my fellatio technique. I was standing beside the driver's-side window of Drew Gillespie's car; he'd just dropped me off at the Kenyon front gate, and I touched the back of his neck as he held his face in his hands, his forehead against the steering wheel. I was out in California, on top of Mount Tamalpais, at my sister Patricia's wedding, winking at her new husband. I was sitting in K.A.'s office on my second day at Winslow, Cooper, looking at the distant Deco spires of the Chrysler Building and the Empire State. I was with Marshall, skating in the park.

There was no connection. There was no order.

"A guy I knew in high school," I said. "Someone who was in love with me."

"What, was he stalking you?"

"No. I was glad he was there."

"Are you in love with him?"

"I don't know."
"Did you talk to him?"
"Sort of."
"You're being cryptic."
"Don't go back to the office, Claudia."
"This is too weird."

Yes, it was. And I wish I'd sent her out of town. But then she'd have missed the big show.

the sunset faded behind the Capitol dome as I stood in my dark apartment, staring out the bay window and gnawing my nails. The door was locked. I'd looked in every closet, behind every appliance, under the bed. The number of messages on my machine was up to five. Time to play them. Much as I wanted to avoid it.

I pressed the play button.

The first one was from Harvey Gitlin. He really enjoyed

meeting me, and could we get together sometime? That party, only a week in the past, seemed some kind of Mesozoic relic. It was as if the Second Coming had happened in the interim, and we were reckoning time differently now.

One from Claudia: "Lucius wants to see you, whenever you can find the time." Her ironic office assistant mode.

One from Lucius himself: "Where the hell are you? Get in here! Called your cell phone, what's wrong?"

I didn't have a cell phone anymore, that's what was wrong.

Then my blood froze. The accent, unmistakable. "Rosalind, I'm sorry we parted so badly in New York. Call my cellular number, please. You have it, I know."

Van Zyk. He didn't even bother to say his name.

Then a hang-up. Of course.

I started shivering. This was the first wintry night we'd had this year. I felt the old water-circulation radiator next to the window. It was barely warm. I remembered cold mornings in Zanesville, when the five of us girls would pile up in front of the heat register in the bathroom, trying to monopolize the rushing air. Sometimes I would sit alone in the utility closet with the gas furnace, watching the fierce blue flame through the tiny inspection port, crouching in the utter blackness as the rest of the household clangorously scurried to breakfast.

Right now they were sitting down to dinner with their husbands and children.

I still wasn't hungry.

When all the light in the western sky was gone, I locked myself in the bathroom with *The Imitation of Christ*. Now I wished I had that gun Marshall had offered me. A false security, maybe, but something.

Mother would tell me to put my trust in the Virgin Mary.

And then I read:

If you ever saw any man die, remember you must go the same way. In the morning, doubt whether you will live till night; at night, do not think yourself certain to live till morning. Be always ready, and live in such manner that death may not find you unprepared. Remember how many have died suddenly and unprepared, for our Lord called them in the hour they least suspected His summons.

Well, I was on notice, at least.

I got out my mandolin and hit the open double strings: G, D, A, E. I laid my finger across the twelfth fret and chimed those same notes as harmonics. The sound sent me back to my old LPs, to another record from my Kenyon days. Bill Monroe. A keening, minor-key instrumental called "My Last Days on Earth." The song began and ended with sounds of seabirds. I tried to think of the ocean, of green fields, of Morpheus carrying me into deep velveteen sleep.

It didn't work. I couldn't sleep. I might never sleep again, I thought.

I couldn't stay in my apartment. I changed into jeans and a sweater and put a tweed jacket on top of that. Then I packed a small gym bag, enough to see me through a night in a hotel. In the inside pocket of my jacket I carried the envelope with Marshall's posthumous instructions. Out on East Capitol I looked around. Here I am, I thought. Go ahead and do it.

I walked south on Third Street, toward the bars and restaurants on Pennsylvania Avenue. I'd be safe there. But I ended up walking past Pennsylvania, south into the realms of quiet again, down where someone could unobtrusively dispatch me with a knife or a silenced pistol. Finally I turned around and walked back north, but before I got back to Pennsylvania I turned west on C Street. And there stood St. Peter's, the Catholic church I'd gone to once or twice, for old times' sake. The evening Mass had already let out, and the huge sanctuary was deserted. I stood behind the back pew, looking up at bloody Jesus hanging in midair over the altar. CHRIST HAS DIED, it said on one side of the apse; CHRIST HAS RISEN, it said on the other. Candles to the Virgin Mother were burning in the corners behind me. Finally I walked around into the pew, lowered the kneeler, and for the first time since I was fourteen assumed the posture of abjection and without irony prayed.

ONCE I WAS in a hotel bed, I did finally sleep. For some reason I fled to Woodley Park, toward danger rather than away from it. But when I walked out in the morning light, all the previous evening's fear and paranoia began to dissipate. It's hard to walk the peaceful, leafy streets of Northwest Washington and keep the world's dark side in view. So as a reminder I strolled up Cathedral to Marshall's house. There was still a strip of yellow police tape across the front door. I kept walking. For hours, as it happened. I was afraid that if I stopped moving, I would float away, or collapse in a heap of ashes. Spontaneously combust. From Cathedral I walked up Woodley to Klingle Road, a street across Rock Creek Park that the city abandoned a few years earlier. They just stopped maintaining it, and Nature was taking it back for herself. Vines were stretching across the cracked pavement; the concrete under the asphalt was showing in places; it was a glimpse of the future, should things break down for even a short period. It was also one of the most relaxing places in Washington, an unplanned urban oasis. There's something about ruins. Even a ruin as unprepossessing as a crumbling road.

Of course I was aware that by moving into this deserted terrain I was making it easy on anyone who might be trailing me. At one point the road passed under Connecticut Avenue, and I looked up at the vaulted arch of the stone bridge. There were many good places to die here. I ducked behind a tree and waited, watching the road. After about twenty minutes a jogger appeared, probably someone exercising on his lunch hour. Guy in an Amherst sweatshirt. I let him run by and resumed my journey.

Up through the park to the neighborhood around Blagden Avenue, then down Sixteenth to Mount Pleasant, then Adams-Morgan. Thinking about my father and the connections with Langford and Lucius and Van Zyk. Since 1979. While I was in junior high, putting on my first support bra, my father was taking Trevor Langford's money from Lucius Atkinson and putting it out in his scams. Nineteen seventy-nine. That was the year I first noticed Drew. He was a year ahead of me in school, the boy with the Telecaster, one of the names girls wrote on their notebook covers. I was a name, too, but on the boys' bathroom wall. By the time Drew and I connected, Lucius was gone. He'd moved on, to Rigel Associates, which launched the same year I graduated from high school. The beginning of Ronald Reagan's second term. By 1988, the cops were watching my dad. The pinch was coming. As it comes for us all, one way or another.

It was late afternoon by the time I stood before my old group house on Calvert Street. The one I'd lived in for a year before moving to New York and starting law school. We were all kids in our early twenties, smoking and laughing and avoiding the future. Who'd have known? That I'd stand here ten years later, a witness to murder and the target of assassins? Of course if we knew what was coming in life, we'd never get out of bed. Only one thing in life is certain. And some people think they can beat that.

I felt the envelope in the inside pocket of my jacket.

Just across the bridge was Rigel's uptown office. Marshall's old hideaway. Of course I had a key. I faced myself west and put one foot in front of the other. In the middle of the bridge I stopped and looked down at the pebble bed of Rock Creek, at the glinting riffles on the water surface. The city—in thrall to the bogus cult of the therapeutic and an unfortunately justified fear of litigation—had put up an ugly high railing as a suicide barrier, spoiling what had been the most beautiful bridge in Washington.

For a long time I stood there.

At last, as it was beginning to get dark again, I walked to the row house where Marshall had his unmarked office. I let myself in, and upstairs I punched a security code. For some reason I was not anxious to open that strongbox. A reluctant Pandora. I almost expected to see Van Zyk sitting in Marshall's chair. But it was empty. I sat down in it myself, enjoying the feel, swiveling back and forth. I'd never been in this chair. I'd only been under the desk.

I turned on the computer. Most of the files were accessible using the common Rigel password. I recognized the directory headings, the same ones on my computer, the ones listing our major clients and partners. American Electric Power. Darius Energy. Siemans. Enron. British Petroleum. Cryolon AFC International. No surprises there. Then I opened the Xantex file. The one I'd seen on Lucius's computer that night. The one with the locked subdirectories. The password prompt blinked at me, waiting. I tried a few of the shared passwords. Of course none of them worked.

There was one subdirectory, also locked, that hadn't been on Lucius's machine.

"Revolving Facility," it said.

Outside, it was nearly dark. I twirled the chair and looked at my reflection in the window. Did Marshall really love me?

I turned back to the machine, to the blinking password prompt.

I typed in a name: ROSALIND.

I hit the enter key and watched the screen part like the Red Sea. A new directory appeared, listing three files. The first file was named "Augustine." I'd come back to that. The next file, called "Sources," had a subdirectory of city names. Sofia. Medellín. Bogotá. São Paulo. Buenos Aires. Lagos. Bangkok. Johannesburg.

I opened Sofia.

A string of Bulgarian names. Or Russian. And a list of revenues. Counterfeit CDs: $39 million. Counterfeit videos: $14 million. Pharmaceuticals: $77 million. Oil & Gas: $43 million.

Pharmaceuticals. Nice euphemism.

I scrolled through the entries. On and on. And the same for the other cities, the only notable changes being the counterfeit clothing number for Bangkok and the diamond money from Johannesburg. There was a list of foreign banks, all new to me. A string of cable addresses in the Cayman Islands. And a payout record I'd never seen: $30 million, plus nickels and dimes, to Executive Resources for unspecified "services."

That was it. The capital sources for the Xantex investment pool. Dirty money from all over the world, multiculturalism triumphant. The Brits, meaning Arlie Ralston and Trevor Langford, must have had a falling-out. A disagreement over management philosophy, perhaps. And it spilled over on their American lackeys, the principals at Rigel Associates.

I exited that file and opened "Augustine." Here the numbers were much smaller, hundreds of thousands of dollars instead of millions. The categories were "rents," "interest," and—once again—"pharmaceuticals." There was no mention of my father's name. But there was something interesting: the transaction record ended in 1994, the year my father vanished.

I scrolled up and down the document. The last entry was May 1994: $72,000, under "interest." Then there was a notation: "account closed, assets transferred." The pretransfer balance was $1,867,542.

I wondered if that was the transfer that so interested Van Zyk.

The last file was labeled "BDSI." It was a one-line document, a sixteen-digit account number and a balance figure, $3,744,553.00. The exact sum I found missing from the Xantex escrow account that morning last month. The morning of my dream.

My hands were shaking. BDSI, of course, was Banca della Svizzera Italiana. And the account number—well, we'd see. I pulled the card Drew gave me out of my wallet. The card my father passed to him at the end of the trial, the day my dad was convicted of bribery, extortion, and illegal distribution of narcotics. They hadn't yet gotten around to trying him for wire fraud and tax evasion. Not to mention pending civil suits for tortious conversion and breach of contract. Those trials would have to be in absentia.

The numbers matched. Marshall's secret Swiss account and my father's were one and the same account.

I looked at the card in my hand. I turned it over and read my father's name. Then I wrote the number down on a piece of Marshall's stationery and stuck it in my brassiere. So I had it twice. Then I had a different idea: I pulled the paper out of my bra and set it afire with my cigarette lighter. I held it as it burned and finally let the ash remnant drop into the wastebasket. I took my father's card, sealed it in an envelope, and addressed it to my mother in Cincinnati. There were stamps in Marshall's desk.

Lucius wasn't my father's secret partner. It was Marshall.

What was Marshall thinking? That he would hide this money and we'd use it to run away together? That he'd play ball with the FBI, get a reduced sentence, then tell me the story when he got out?

At the National Gallery he'd talked about a trip. Just the two of us. To Laos, maybe. Was my father there, waiting in the jungle for his money and his daughter?

I might never know, I thought.

Whatever the story was, the money hadn't moved. If my father, wherever he was, had access, he wasn't letting on.

I took Marshall's letter out of my pocket.

Following the instructions, I went to the walnut closet with louvered doors and found the strongbox in the back left corner. I struggled to pull it out. It was small but heavy. After three tries at the combination I opened the lid.

It wasn't diamonds or gold coins.

It was two Argentine passports, along with visa papers for Lao PDR. Laos, I gathered. There was a card, with a P.O. box address in Vientiane. A name I didn't recognize. A foreign name, probably Laotian. I looked at the passports. One had a picture of Marshall, but the name was Lowell Varney. The other one had a picture of me. It was my official general counsel photo for Rigel Associates. But my name was Anne Thornton. I wondered what the private significance of that name could have been.

I ran my finger over his face. So now I knew. When was he going to tell me?

There was something else in the box. A letter. I recognized the handwriting. It was my father's. This letter was not to me. It was to Marshall. Dated September 1994.

> *Marshall,*
>
> *It appears we can help each other. If you're determined to get back to Laos. Get me the Argentine travel papers, and I'll give you a place to park your funds. So you clean up your mines and nurse your sick children. Whatever that fantasy is. I may stay in Buenos Aires. But the courts could decline my appeals any day now, and then it's the slammer. So I'd prefer to have made all my arrangements before then. Ciao.*

I knelt by the strongbox, reading and rereading the letter.

I loaded the passports and the letter into my overnight bag. I put the card with the Laotian name and address into another stamped envelope addressed to my mother.

Marshall had been planning to flee to Laos as early as 1994, four years before I met him. But he hadn't. And he hadn't wanted me to come to the firm. It wasn't convenient. His partners wanted my father to pay his debts to the firm, but Marshall had his own agenda. He didn't want me to be hired, but he couldn't appear to object. It wouldn't look right, his not wanting to collect. Then his plans changed. He changed them to include me.

Then everything changed. Before he could tell me what was on his mind.

I ran my life through my mind again, the way I had in Lincoln Park. There was an order, after all.

I closed the strongbox. Let them drill it, just to find it empty.

I sat back down at the computer. I deleted the BDSI file, going through the elaborate procedure of wiping it not only from the directory but from the hard drive itself.

The phone rang. I snapped back so hard I almost turned over the chair. There was no answering machine connected to this phone. I let it ring. That's the hardest thing in the world to do. Why is that? After seventeen rings it stopped.

It occurred to me that I had been unreachable since I left my apartment last night. Almost twenty-four hours ago. I had no cell phone. I could check my home messages. I could do that from a pay phone. I didn't want to do it from this phone. I didn't want a record of anyone having been here.

On Connecticut Avenue I dropped the envelopes in a mailbox and dialed up my messages at a public phone. There were two, both from Claudia. She was back at the office. And I'd *ordered* her not to go back there! Lucius had to see me, she said. Fuck. Fuck, fuck, fuck. I was so mad I got right in a taxi.

"East Capitol Street," I said. "Near the Folger."

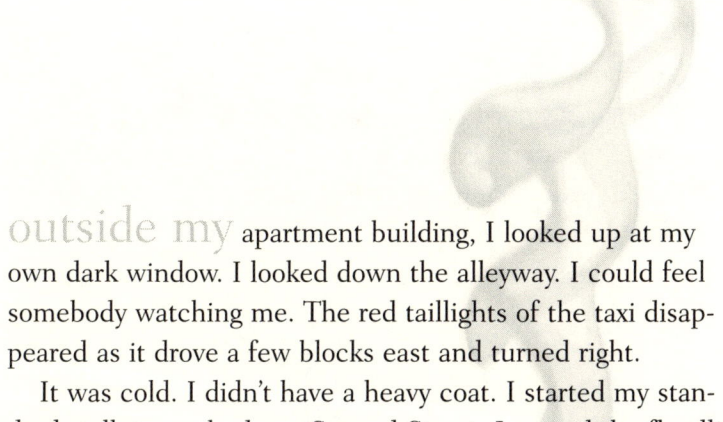

outside my apartment building, I looked up at my own dark window. I looked down the alleyway. I could feel somebody watching me. The red taillights of the taxi disappeared as it drove a few blocks east and turned right.

It was cold. I didn't have a heavy coat. I started my standard walk to work, down Second Street. I passed the floodlit back of the Supreme Court, with the inscription JUSTICE, THE GUARDIAN OF LIBERTY high on the pediment. No one was on the street. One or two stars were visible over the English Gothic battlements of the Rigel building. The upstairs lights were on. Inside the front door, the alarm code was set to allow free entry. I walked up the steps to the second floor. I was ready to beat the shit out of Lucius. I was going to really hurt him this time. Claudia's office light was on, but she wasn't in there. Lucius's door was open. I walked to the threshold.

"Please come in," Van Zyk said. He was holding an automatic pistol, a Beretta from the look of it, with a silencer screwed on the barrel.

"Hi, Roos."

Immediately to my left, Claudia sat with her back against the wall, her wrists and ankles tied with computer coax. She looked at me from over the silver duct tape covering her mouth. She'd been crying. To my right, sitting upright at his desk, like the honor student he once was, Lucius stared morosely at the opposite wall. His mouth was taped, too. For once he was silent. Thank God for small favors.

"Working through your feelings about Americans, Roos?"

Claudia mumbled something behind her gag.

"I was hoping you'd come," Van Zyk said. "I wasn't sure the phone messages from your assistant would suffice."

"Claudia wasn't supposed to be here."

"I brought her here myself. Picked her up at her apartment. We had a little date, you might say."

"You piece of shit."

"Be nice. We have business to conduct."

"You got her to call me."

"She did a fine job."

"You fucking bastard."

"As I said, we need to get down to business."

"You seem to have already been pretty busy."
"They were pretty cooperative, considering."
"What are you talking about?"
"I got the pooftah here to tie up the girl for me."
I didn't say anything.
"Did a pretty fair job, don't you agree?"
"I suppose."
"I made some adjustments."
"And now what?"
"Well, now I want you to help me with something."
"What?"
"I haven't found what I was looking for."

A funny thought came into my head: Van Zyk had been a little boy once. I glanced at Lucius and thought the same thing. He'd once looked up from Freud and Marcuse at the high coffered ceiling of Butler Library and wondered why he was on this earth, why there was a war going on, what did it all mean. Well, he still didn't have his answers. Or if he did, I wasn't going to have to listen to them. Not right now, anyway.

"And what are you looking for, Roos?"
"Some computer files. And I think you know where they are."
"I'm sure I don't."
"Now, how can you be sure of that? I haven't even told you what they are."
"All right. Tell me."
"I know Marshall had another office. I just never knew where."
"This is our office. Right here."
"He had another one. Never mind denying it. You're going to take me there."

"I don't know about another office."

"Sure you do. You know everything about Marshall. You turned his head. You undermined our whole operation, you little subversive. You surprised everyone. Especially Marshall."

"You're nuts."

"I have the feeling you know your way around some Swiss accounts, too. But we'll have time to talk about that. At our leisure."

I was suddenly glad I'd taken that paper out of my bra.

"Where's Trevor?" I asked.

"Well, there's been another management shuffle."

"You killed him."

"Nothing so melodramatic. Rigel Associates is going out of business. I'm just restructuring our deal."

"What do you intend to do with us?"

"My car's right outside. Now turn around."

I just looked at him. I was sure he was getting ready to shoot Lucius and Claudia, but I didn't know what to do.

"I said turn around."

As I did, a shadow appeared in the doorway. Van Zyk saw it the same time I did, and he grabbed me from behind. The shadow came through the door, holding out a .45. I'd seen it before.

"Hold it!" said Drew Gillespie.

"Drew."

Van Zyk had his arm around my throat and the silencer pressed against my temple. I was pulling uselessly on his forearm. I could feel his tremendous strength.

"Idiot," Van Zyk said. "Stupid jackass. Put down the gun."

"No."

"Drop it."

"No, you drop it."

"I'll shoot her. You know you can't hit me."

I was in a position I'd been in too many times: stuck between two men.

"I can try."

"Put it down."

Drew lowered his arm.

"Put it on safety and put it down."

Drew thumbed the safety and set the pistol down on the edge of Lucius's desk.

"All right," said Van Zyk. "We were just about to take a ride. But you can't go. Kneel down."

"No."

"Kneel down."

I kicked Van Zyk's shin and tried to wriggle from his grasp. It didn't work. He held me tighter and bashed the side of my head with his gun. In my white flash of agony I tried to kick backward again, aiming for his balls. No go. My vision was blacking out.

Drew charged. Van Zyk shot him point-blank, the sound so muffled by the silencer that I wasn't sure at first what had happened. Drew took us all down in a flying tackle, and Van Zyk let go of me. The gun went off again. Drew was holding Van Zyk's wrist against the floor. Of course Drew was a strong boy himself. I remembered that very well.

I kicked the Beretta out of Van Zyk's hand, and it flew into the corner, out of reach. I backed away as they rolled around, grasping at each other's throat. Drew's .45 was just a short grab for me. I picked it up and pointed it, trying to stop my hands from shaking.

"Get up," I said to Van Zyk.

He sat back, breathing hard, and Drew curled into a ball.

Blood was spreading from his stomach. Claudia was moaning, and for a moment I was afraid she'd been shot. But she hadn't been.

"Get up," I said again.

"You don't know what you're doing," said Van Zyk.

"I know what I'm going to do."

"Don't make this harder than it has to be."

"Get away from him. Stand up."

Eventually he did stand up.

"Slowly," I said.

"You're in over your head," he said.

I slid the safety off with my thumb. The hammer was already back. I knew what he was thinking. It was a reasonable presumption on his part: that an American woman of a certain education would have no familiarity with this thing I was holding.

"Back against the wall," I said. My voice quavered. I hated hearing that. I held the gun with both hands, to stop my shaking. Straight up and down. None of that Hollywood horseshit of holding the pistol sideways, some production designer's idea of how to shoot a gun.

"You're clueless," he said. "You've always been clueless."

He was giving me *that look*. The look I'd seen all my life. *You're just a girl,* the look said. I was conscious of Claudia and Lucius watching me.

"Put the gun down, bitch."

Those were his last words. I wish I could control my temper, but I can't.

we're three miles east of Cumberland, Maryland, doing sixty-five on I-68, headed into the sinking sun. Drew's asleep beside me, here in the cab of his '67 Ford pickup. It's December, the shortest day of the year, and we're driving through to Cincinnati. I'm doing the driving. Will be for a while, actually. We'll be spending Christmas with my family. We missed my birthday. And Thanksgiving. Drew was in the hospital, and it didn't look too good for a few days there. For a week or so, he wasn't listed any better than "serious." And there were other distractions. I had to see Claudia off. She left for a long vacation in Barbados, to consider her next step in life. Then there were long sessions with Payson. Talks with the D.C. cops. A visit with one of the district attorney's minions. A real jerk-off. Kept wanting to talk about that third bullet. The fatal one. The limits of self-defense. I really disliked him, but I had to play nice.

I shot Van Zyk three times. And yes, by the third time he was already on the floor. But I could have used up the clip. I guess I'm glad I didn't. It would be that much more to explain. But I liked it, pulling the trigger. I'm not going to lie to you the way I lied to the D.A. (I cried, too. Oh, it was quite a performance.) Thinking of Claudia, I could have pulled that trigger forever. Something stopped me. Maybe it was the sight of Drew, still curled up in agony and needing my attention.

Look at him now, snoring lightly, his mouth open. I like the domestic intimacy of it: this warm cab, the winter dusk outside, the heartland before us. Did he save my life? Maybe. He was following me, all that time after Marshall was killed. He knew I was in danger. At night he watched my apartment, and in the daytime he watched my office. He even followed me to New York. He was really worried, he said, when he came up behind me at Arlie Ralston's murder scene. The cops might have noticed him, and he was carrying a gun. It would have been very sticky. And he was behind me that last day, when I was wandering all over town and I ended up at Marshall's office. When I came out the front door and down the steps, he was in the shadows across Calvert Street. I'd surprised him, catching a cab as quickly as I did, and by the time he got to his truck he'd lost me. He first went to my apartment, and only when he found I wasn't home did he go to my office. That's why he was slightly late.

"I'll forgive you for that," I whispered in his unconscious ear, the first night I was allowed to see him, after he'd told me the story and the effort of speaking put him back under.

I said it to him again when he opened his eyes the next day.

"I'm sorry about that first night at the Tabard," I told him when he was finally out of danger in the hospital. "It was a bad time."

"I know."

"You didn't know how bad."

"Neither did you."

"No."

"But we found out."

"Well, I'm really glad you came."

"I should have called first."

"No, you did the right thing. I might have said no."

"I might have come, anyway."

"Actually, I've got a long story to tell you, when you're feeling better."

"About what?"

"About Marshall. And my dad. And that Swiss account. A lot of things."

That Swiss account. With Marshall dead, only my dad knows the authorization codes to move the money.

"Why didn't you tell me you were in trouble when I first came to Washington?"

"I was mad."

"Why?"

"Because my dad gave that Swiss account number to you and not to me."

"Maybe he knew I would give it to you."

"I should have told you everything."

"How long were you going to wait?"

"I don't know. Till the right time came."

We laughed at the same moment. I took his hand and didn't let go of it until he was asleep again. After that I was at his bedside every day. We didn't talk about this trip. It was simply a given that, when he finally got up, we would drive away together.

It's not as if I'll miss Washington. I saved enough of my fat general counsel's salary to retire my law school debt. I've exhausted whatever curiosity I may have had about coming to work in a suit. I've learned a few things.

Here's one of them: the latte life is not worth living.

They arrested Trevor Langford out at Dulles as he was trying to board a flight to Buenos Aires. He wasn't dead, after all. He had an Executive Resources corporate credit card and an Argentine passport identifying him as Jaime Cortazar. There are plenty of Brits in Argentina, but he was the palest Cortazar the customs people had ever encountered. But they already knew he was wanted. They were waiting for him.

Payson was happy. My supplying the password to the Calvert Street computer files saved him a few days of hacker hassle. He never asked me if any files had been erased. Nor did he mention a certain Swiss account. He seemed to still be laboring under the impression that Van Zyk moved the money and that it may be lost. Lucius has been a nonstop canary, trying to keep his hide out of prison. He talks and talks and talks, I've heard. It's a gift. But he's left Payson's ideas about the escrow account undisturbed. It was a promise I extracted from him before I pulled the tape off his mouth. So far it's held.

Xantex led to a string of Cayman Islands corporate entities now under investigation for tax evasion and money laundering. Payson gets a promotion, sometime next year. He promised to do his best to avoid calling me back for Langford's murder trial. I'm going to hold him to that. Of course we had to give up Drew's gun. The Combat Commander I used to shoot Van Zyk. Drew was carrying it illegally. He'd had it for years—I remembered it from the strip mine days—and was sad to lose it, but the cops were kind not to charge him. Drew was a .45 partisan. That was one of the raps I used to have to listen to: that the new nine millimeters sucked. Real men stuck with the .45.

We're coming up on the exit to Highway 40, north into Pennsylvania. There's only a little light left. Drew murmurs something in his sleep, gripped by Tylenol 3. I'm looking forward to my vintage Thunderbird.

Back in high school he had a black Malibu SS. He'd taken out the "gutless" 285 engine and dropped in a 312. It's coming back to me now, the things he did to it: the four-barrel carburetor, the glass-pack mufflers. The Hurst shifter. Extra gauges. There was one on the steering column, I remember, for water temperature. And a tachometer, of course. We rode in that thing for hours. And once, for days. We took a road trip to New Orleans. Down across Kentucky and Tennessee and Mississippi. Summer of '84, the summer after I graduated. He'd already been out for a year, had gone to Alaska and come back. We headed off together. The two-lane blacktop giving off a tar smell, and the green overgrowth like a wall on either side of the road. We came into New Orleans on that long low bridge across the Pontchartrain, I had one leg out the window, and we had a fight over the AC/DC tape that I wanted to replace with the Clash. Later we were in a bar in the French Quarter, sort of a biker joint, and Drew decided to play the big man and challenge the local patrons to high-stakes pool matches. High stakes by our standards, considering we only had about two hundred dollars. I was a great accessory, lolling like a moll and chatting up the bartender. "How come these guys all look alike?" I whispered. "Do they have the same mother?" He laughed and gave me a free beer. Which was convenient, because Drew lost all our money. It was so romantic. He lost our money, we had a public screaming fight on Royal Street, and he drove off without me. Left me, broke and alone.

Washington, Pa.: 22 miles.

Of course he came back for me. He knew I wouldn't be alone long. We had a great time making up. Somewhere in Tennessee we pulled off a back road and went skinny-dipping. It was a gravel-bottomed creek under a railroad trestle. A hot August afternoon. I looked down at Drew, standing in waist-deep water just outside the latticed shadow of the trestle. As I pushed off the bank and swam toward him, he backed up into shallower water, took his pecker in his two hands, and waggled it at me. I crawled toward him, grinding my knees in the gravel, biting the air while he danced around teasing me. Later we made love standing in a neck-deep pool. Looking over Drew's shoulder, my legs locked around his waist, I saw a water moccasin swimming upstream.

I reach over now and touch his cheek.

Souls on a journey.

It's completely dark now. We're entering Washington, Pennsylvania, a town I've seen before. Just on the other side we slide onto I-70, the straight shot to Zanesville and points beyond. The road whose two-lane predecessor my dad must have thumbed his way down in 1948, leaving Pittsburgh forever. The launch on the trajectory he's still charting, destination unknown. I'll pass the way he did: through Wheeling, by Zanesville, on to Columbus. Then south.

He's out there somewhere, my dad. And I'm going to find him. It's my next project. Just as soon as Drew is back on his feet. I'm going to head out looking. I'm sending a letter to a certain P.O. box in Vientiane. There may be a trip to Argentina. I'm going to settle that pool they're running in Zanesville. Whatever it takes. He's out there, an outrider on his strange streets, but he won't be alone. I'll be with him, like a clot in his veins, racing to catch him in the chambers of his heart.